As Good As It Gets

MARG MCALISTER

BLUE GEM PUBLISHING

This edition published by Blue Gem Publishing in 2022.

Title: As Good as it Gets | Marg McAlister, author

ISBN: 978-1-922772-34-3 (Paperback edition)

ISBN: 978-0-9945205-6-2 (Ebook edition)

Cover Design by Annie Moril

V27032022

CHAPTER 1

Callaway's Flying Circus

"Wow," Georgie said, staring down at the explosion of color in the field below. "I didn't know it was so big."

"It wasn't always," Scott said. "But that's what winning twenty-seven million will do."

Georgie's gaze tracked across the bright tents, the gaily painted RVs and trailers, the striped Big Top, the sideshows, the giant sign that sat over the wide entrance bordered by neat white picket fences: *Callaway's Flying Circus*. Underneath that, in slightly smaller letters, written in italic font, were the words "*& Carnival*".

"How many people work here?"

"Not sure. Fifty? Sixty? Plus the kids."

"Wow," she said again. "I always wanted to run away and join the circus. Doesn't every kid?"

Scott laughed. "Performing as what? A clown? Bearded lady?"

"I did gymnastics until I was ten," Georgie said, taking a swipe at him. "I wasn't exactly one of the stars, but who knows? With training, I could have been a trapeze artist. Maybe." Then her eye measured the size of the Big Top, and she thought about how she had never been any good with heights. "Or maybe not."

Behind them, the sound of a motor grew closer, and there was a crunch of gravel as a vehicle pulled off the road and stopped behind her gypsy trailer. She could tell it was Jerry's motorhome before she turned around.

Tammy was following close behind, towing her vintage trailer. She pulled off the road too, and they both got out to join Georgie and Scott.

Tammy came to stand beside Georgie. "Wow."

"That's what I said," agreed Georgie. "It looks amazing."

Jerry stood behind Tammy, with his hands on her shoulders. "Just think, we built half of those RVs and trailers. And Rollo Callaway is so thrilled with them he tells the whole world he bought them from Johnny B. Goode. You can't pay for that kind of advertising."

"I always wanted to join the circus," Tammy said, making Georgie laugh.

"See?" she said, elbowing Scott. "*Everyone* wants to do it at some time."

They stood for another few moments, drinking it in. Georgie could feel the same excitement she'd always felt as a kid when a circus or carnival came to town. Death-defying aerial acts, noise and music, the thrill of the amusement rides. Callaway's Flying Circus (& Carnival) didn't have any rides; it focused on performance arts and sideshows: trapeze artists, tumbling, trampoline, aerial silk, contortionists, stilt walkers, and fire eaters. And, of course, clowns and jugglers who did tricks and joined in the tumbling and gymnastics. Then there were the sideshows and booths: knife throwing, an illusionist, shooting gallery, knock em downs, and food stands.

Callaway's Circus also had a gypsy fortune-teller.

A gypsy fortune-teller who was, apparently, not much good at what she did. She was the reason Georgie had been asked to come along.

Her gaze moved to the lone gypsy trailer parked at the end of sideshow alley, between the sideshows and the fenced-off row of RVs and trailers that were the circus folks' home on the road.

Georgie gave a small sigh. How could you *train* someone to tell the future?

She had her doubts about whether it could be done at all, but the Callaways were paying the Johnny B. Goode RV Empire vast sums of money to get everything right—including giving some tips to their new fortune-teller. So here she was.

Under protest, but here.

"Well," she said, "I guess we'd better go down and meet them all."

"Guess so," agreed Scott, rubbing her upper arm reassuringly. "She might be just like you. You didn't know anything before Rosa gave you her crystal ball."

"Mmf," Georgie said, thinking instead about Rosa's mother, her great-great-grandmother. She had cheerfully made up fortunes just to earn money without being able to see any further than that night's dinner menu. What if this girl was just the same?

She *couldn't* be a party to promoting a fake fortune-teller.

"We'll see," she said. "Let's go find the Callaways."

Theodora Callaway was tall, loud, and dramatic. A swinging bell of chin-length hair, colored a defiant rich red, formed a contrast to the sweeping dark wings of her eyebrows and the bright blue of her eyes. She moved with the grace of a former dancer, but Georgie guessed that she had probably once been a gymnast like the rest of the family.

Jerry and Tammy had met the Callaways several times before, working with them on design and fit-out. Georgie could feel her brother's eyes on her, with barely-concealed amusement, when he introduced her to Theodora.

"Ah, you're the fortune-teller!" she boomed, extending a hand bedecked in rings and jangling silver bracelets. "Excellent. Ginger needs a guiding hand. I've always felt that she had a gift, but she won't listen." She clapped Georgie on the shoulder. "You'll sort her out."

Georgie smiled. "I look forward to meeting her."

A voice, tinged with annoyance and resentment, broke in. "I'm right here, Mom. You don't have to talk about me as though I'm some kid in the naughty corner."

Theodora gave an exaggerated start. "Ginger! I didn't see you there."

"Yeah, right." A slightly built woman with

strawberry-blonde hair caught back in a braid moved in from the fringes of the swelling group of Callaways. They were flooding from everywhere, attracted by the arrival of a new gypsy trailer and the big black and gold Johnny B. Goode motorhome piloted by Jerry. Tammy's cheerful red and white vintage trailer was attracting its share of admiring glances, too, although nobody seemed very interested in Scott's humble truck camper.

Ginger narrowed her eyes at Georgie, not offering a hand. "I'm Ginger, and this is all Mom's bright idea."

Georgie kept her voice mild. "I'm not pushing anything at you, Ginger. Let's just talk and see where it leads." She smiled at her. "Fortune-telling isn't for everyone."

Theodora raised a finger and stabbed in the general direction of the circus's brand new gypsy trailer. "Too late. We've got the gypsy wagon waiting." She cast a quelling look at her daughter. "You can't do the aerial work anymore, so it might as well be fortune-telling."

Georgie felt her hackles rise, and her smile faded. It "might as well be fortune-telling"? She didn't mind it when people challenged her on what she did, but she *did* mind when they relegated the

Sight to a low-grade parlor trick. Feeling Ginger's eyes on her, she held back from a retort.

What had happened to stop Ginger from doing aerial work? She'd have to find out.

A man with the same general body shape as Ginger edged around Theodora to introduce himself. He vibrated with energy, almost bouncing on his feet. "I'm Rollo Callaway," he said, grinning. His eyes were hazel and kind, with deep laughter lines. "General manager and go-fer, husband of Theodora, father of Ginger, Darcy, Cassandra, and Oscar." He pointed at each one of his children as he said their names. "Since you're here for the week, you'll get to know them."

Georgie and Scott shook hands, nodded, and smiled as they worked their way around the group. The only one of the children to echo his mother's height was Darcy, who was dark and athletic, with an aerialist's knotted shoulder muscles. He shared Theodora's bright blue eyes, as did the youngest daughter Cassandra. Like her father, Cassandra radiated energy. "Our star performer," Rollo said proudly, patting his daughter on the head. "What she can't do with aerial silk, nobody can."

Georgie didn't miss the quick flash of hurt in Ginger's eyes at the words and her sideways glance at her brother Oscar, who was standing patiently waiting for the introductions to end. He seemed to be a miniature version of his father, but still and quiet. He put his hand briefly on Ginger's arm, an empathetic touch.

Interesting family dynamics.

"And these two are my two of our newest additions, Angelique and her brother Travis," Rollo went on. "Good all-round performers, both of them, but Angelique excels on the high wire while Travis does aerial silk and tumbling."

Blonde Angelique gave a brief nod, looking bored, and red-haired Travis stepped forward to shake hands with an engaging smile.

"Might as well do the tour," Rollo went on, flinging out an arm to encompass the entire circus. "Come on; I'll show you around. After all these years, we've finally made it." His face shone with pride. "This, folks, would have to be as good as it gets!"

The next hour passed in a whirl of being introduced to other performers and laborers and a whole bunch of assorted children as they toured the circus setup, from Theodora and Rollo's 1.3 million dollar RV to the Big Top. Then every booth from the hot dog stand to the cotton candy machine.

Finally, Rollo ran out of steam. "You'll be wanting to set up," he said. "Jerry, after you've had a break, come find me." He grinned. "You know where I live. I'll give you a list of the fixes we need —perhaps we can get started on those in the morning? Our first performance is tomorrow night, and then it's a busy week until we move on."

"Sure," Jerry said easily. "Unless there's anything urgent you want me to look at before dinner?"

Rollo nodded. "The water pump in Cassandra's bathroom, maybe, and the general drainage there. There's a leak. The rest can wait until tomorrow. You'll join us for a cookout tonight?"

"Thanks." After a glance around, Jerry accepted on behalf of all of them. "OK, I'll come and see you soon."

They all dispersed, but in the background, Georgie could see Ginger leaning against the hot dog stand with her arms folded, watching them.

She did not look happy.

CHAPTER 2

I see Meatloaf

Georgie decided to use some free time to wind down while Scott went with Jerry to look at the water pump problem. Snuggling back into the plump jewel-colored cushions on her bed, with the soft tones of ambient music playing in the background, she stared up at the embossed ceiling of her trailer. The Callaway family interested her. What would it be like to have to pack up a whole circus and move every week or two? Big job.

When a soft knock sounded on the door, she was half-asleep. Jerking awake, she swung her feet to the floor. "Come in."

The door opened slowly to reveal Ginger. She looked chagrined when she saw Georgie sitting on the rumpled bed. "Oh, I'm sorry. You're resting. After that long drive…"

"Don't be silly." Georgie summoned up a welcoming smile, swiftly processing the furrow between Ginger's eyes and the tense set of her shoulders. "I'm glad you came to find me." She gestured at the velvet-upholstered seat at the table and stood up. "Have you got a few minutes to talk?"

Ginger nodded, looking around at the carving, the gauzy curtains tied back at each end of the bed, the stained glass in the windows. "This is nice," she said, obviously making an effort to be pleasant. "Do you live in it permanently?"

"More or less. I'm part of the RV Empire road team." She laughed. "I know you know what *that's* like."

"The gypsy lifestyle. I've never known anything else. I must say it's improved, though, since Dad won the lottery. Bigger RVs all-round, more conveniences, everything new." She sat down. "He's been very generous with all of us. Enough so that I could give it all away now, if I wanted; settle down with my little girl. Give her a real home." Her laugh was tinged with bitterness. "But this is his dream come true; enough money to pay decent performers and have a circus that looks prosperous and polished. If I left now, it'd be like thumbing my nose at him."

Georgie thought back to when she had told her

father that she didn't want to work with him anymore—that she'd rather go on the road, indulging her love of the retro lifestyle. That hadn't been easy, and she knew he still missed having her around the giant Johnny B. Goode RV Empire, even though he had an excellent design team. "I know what you mean," she said. "I disappointed Dad when I broke away from the business."

Ginger cocked her head on one side. "But I thought you were still part of it?"

"Oh, I am, I guess. I'm on the road team, but I'm fairly free to do my own thing." She hesitated. "Which, in my case, is traveling in a gypsy trailer, staying connected with the retro community, and exploring the gift my great-grandmother passed on to me. The Sight." Her eyes met Ginger's. "I didn't want it, and I hadn't planned on it, even though she insisted I had to carry on from her. So I understand your reluctance."

Some of the tension left Ginger's eyes. "You're not offended?"

"Not a bit. If you don't think it's for you, you shouldn't do it."

Ginger slumped and closed her eyes, exhaling a huge sigh. "Thank God. Thank *God.*"

With a pang of sympathy, Georgie patted her on the hand. "Let's talk this out." She glanced at her watch. "It's only four o'clock, but what the heck. Would you like a glass of wine?"

"Yes," Ginger said fervently. "Oh yes. And then you can tell me how the hell I'm going to get out of this."

Georgie sent her a wry grin. "That bad, huh?"

"That bad."

"OK." Georgie poured two glasses of Sauvignon Blanc, added ice to hers, and sat opposite Ginger. The other woman looked a little less defensive, but nerves had her playing with her braid.

"Where should we begin?" Diving in, Georgie went on, "Your mother said you weren't doing aerial work anymore—did something happen?"

"I can't do it. I just can't." Ginger reached for the wine and sipped, then took a larger mouthful. "This is nice. Very smooth."

"One of my favorites." Georgie waited until Ginger filled the silence.

"I fell," she said. "Badly. Fractured an arm in two places, head injuries, broken femur. It took months to heal, and now I just can't bring myself to go back up." The expression in her eyes darkened. "You have to be able to trust your equipment, and when it let me down…" She hunched her shoulders. "I've had falls before, plenty of them. But nothing like this. And I thought, what if

I'd died? Or I'd been paralyzed? Lucy, my little girl, is only six." Seemingly reading Georgie's thoughts, she added neutrally, "No father around."

Georgie nodded, thinking of the high-wire walkers she had watched rehearsing a short time before. "I can understand your reluctance. Just one look at the height you guys work at was enough for me."

"We're used to it. It never worried me before. But once you've been hurt, well." She sipped again. "We all have to pull our weight here, so I had to find something else to do. Mom came up with the fortune-telling idea. She saw the gypsy trailers back at the RV Empire, and that was it." She mimicked Theodora's booming tones. "Ginger, it's finally come to me what you can do. Fortune-telling! It's perfect! You can sit down all day and rest that leg, and I *know* you have a gift."

Georgie let out an appreciative crack of laughter. "You sound just like her."

A hint of guilt showed in Ginger's eyes. "We can all send up Mom. She's an easy target. She's great, in a lot of ways, don't get me wrong. It's just that, well, it's hard to change her mind once she's got a bee in her bonnet."

"And do *you* think you have a gift?"

"I'm intuitive, I guess. I can read people pretty well. But see the future? Come *on*."

The best way to determine that, Georgie thought, was to see what happened when she got out the crystal ball. Even that wasn't definitive, of course: people felt comfortable with different media. Scott and his mother liked to read cards—and in his mother's case, work out astrological charts—and others cast runes or used sticks. It depended on how strong Ginger's 'intuition' was. It might be possible to make something of it.

She stood up. "I meant what I said about no pressure," she reassured Ginger, "but let me get the crystal ball just to see what happens."

She lifted it down from its shelf and put it on the table between them, folding the black velvet cloth used to protect it. It seemed a little duller than usual—or was that just her imagination?

"Just relax. Let's both just think about your situation and see if anything comes up."

Ginger sucked in a deep breath and stared at the crystal ball.

"Don't expect anything. Just empty your mind."

She nodded but kept her gaze fixed.

Georgie let her mind drift while keeping one eye on Ginger and the other on the crystal sphere in front of her. Images of the people she had met that morning floated through her consciousness. Some of them, she could put a name to: primarily members of the Callaway family. Ginger's sister Cassandra, the aerial silk expert with the bright blue eyes; her tall, dark brother Darcy, quiet Oscar…and little Lucy, who shared her mother's ginger hair.

Angelique's face flashed in front of her, the blond performer who had looked so bored. She was trouble, Georgie felt. The demanding type. Self-centered… and yes, Angelique's brother Travis was much the same, despite his cheerful face and dazzling smile. Surprising, she thought, that she hadn't picked that up when introduced to him.

The faces of Angelique and Travis faded, and a dark shadow formed where they had been. A warning, to watch over them? Or to watch *them* closely? Darkness tended to presage a threat of some kind, but she had no idea what.

Abruptly, Ginger's words sounded clearly in her mind: *You have to be able to trust your equipment. What if I'd died?*

A chill snaked up her spine. The cold feeling intensified, and then suddenly, in horror, she understood what she was feeling.

Ginger's accident…*not* just an accident?

Scarcely breathing, she let the knowledge settle while she regained her equilibrium.

Someone in the Callaway Flying Circus was a danger to others who worked there.

Careful not to let anything show on her face, she spoke. "Are you picking up anything at all, Ginger?"

The other woman sighed. "No. My mind keeps wandering to what I'm going to cook for dinner or what Mom's going to say when I tell her I can't do this." She opened her hands in frustration and then pointed at the crystal ball. "Am I supposed to be seeing anything in there?"

"Not necessarily. Even *I* can't always do that." Especially today, Georgie thought. The familiar mist had not formed in the center of the crystal ball. It still looked the same as when she'd uncovered it: a little dull, even in the light from the window. "Sometimes I see things in it; at other times I hear words—and sometimes pictures appear in my mind." She decided to try one more thing. "Try putting your hands on it for a moment, and close your eyes. See if that makes a difference."

Ginger dutifully did so, giving it several moments. Finally, she opened her eyes, took her hands away, and said with a rueful smile: "All I see in my future is meatloaf. Sorry."

Georgie grinned at her. "Did you need a crystal ball for that?"

"Nope."

"OK. Then we'd better start thinking about how we can get around this. How about you give me tonight, let me sleep on it?"

"Sounds good to me." Looking relieved, Ginger stood up. "Thanks for that. I've no idea what I'm going to say to Mom."

"We'll come up with something," Georgie said reassuringly, trying to ignore the sinking feeling in her stomach. She'd as soon face a tank as Theodora.

And how was she going to break the news to the Callaways, who were seeing their dream come true, that there was more to worry about than a daughter who didn't want a career as a fortune-teller?

CHAPTER 3

Tammy Explores

Scott shone a flashlight under the sink in Cassandra's motorhome and played it on the drainage hoses. He moved the beam of light slowly and then let it travel back as he took another look. He reached up, ran his fingers along a pipe, and then stuck his head in further to examine the connections.

Hmm.

Outside, Jerry was sliding out from underneath the RV, his face unreadable. That was enough to tell Scott that he'd found something. That, and the slight narrowing of his eyes.

Seeing Cassandra sprawled in a camp chair nearby, watching, Jerry casually dusted off his hands and sent her a grin. "Hey, Cass—or is it Cassie?"

"Usually, Cassandra," she said. "But some of my friends call me Cass. You can, too." Her gaze swept across Jerry's undeniably impressive physique, and she sat up a little straighter, her bright blue eyes glinting.

"I will." Jerry beamed at her. "Lovely model, this one. We build a nice motorhome if I do say so myself."

"Apart from the pump not working," she said. "And the leak in the bathroom."

"Teething problems. I'll have replacement parts here tomorrow," Jerry promised her. "With a special gift basket to make up for the inconvenience. Meanwhile, we'll fix that leak right away. Right, Scott?"

"As good as done," Scott agreed. "I'll get my tools."

"I'll give you a hand. Back soon, Cass." Jerry sketched a cheerful salute at Cassandra, who had perked up at the idea of a gift basket, and they headed off.

"What did you find?" Jerry asked as soon as they were out of earshot.

"Split hose and tool marks. Either someone's been in trying to fix it, or it's been tampered with."

"Ditto for the pump. And according to Rollo, nobody has tried to fix it because they knew we were coming."

They looked at each other.

"I'll get a replacement pump unit here tomorrow," Jerry said. "You've got tools to fix the problems in the bathroom? Spare hoses?"

"Yeah." Scott thought about it. "Deliberate tampering, you think?"

"Seems that way." Frowning, Jerry stared at the ground while they walked. "Be interesting to see what we find tomorrow with the other problems that have cropped up."

Scott nodded, turning over the possibilities. "Either someone's got a problem with the Callaways, or someone's got a problem with the Johnny B. Goode RV Empire."

They turned to each other with the same thought.

"Maybe we should see what Georgie can find out?" Scott said.

Jerry nodded. "You read my mind."

Scott knew that once, not so long ago, Georgie wouldn't have been the first person Jerry thought of, but he'd had good reason to change his mind since his sister had taken to the road with her great-grandma Rosa's crystal ball. He'd seen plenty now to know he could trust her instincts. Well, more than instinct.

They reached Scott's camper. "I'll take the truck

over there," he said. "We'll fix it first and then find Georgie."

"She just can't stay away from trouble, can she?" Jerry asked. "Everywhere she goes."

Scott shrugged. "She feels that's *why* she ends up in the places she does. She's attracted to them, for some reason, or some unseen force draws her there."

"Not in this case," Jerry said. "All straight down the line. The Callaways ordered a job lot of RVs from us, and the gypsy trailer was part of the deal. Along with training for their fledgling gypsy fortune-teller."

"Who isn't keen."

"Who isn't keen," Jerry agreed.

Then, both together, they said "Hmm…" and exchanged another glance.

"Something else has drawn her here," Scott said again. "You wait and see."

Tammy glanced to the left as she passed the shooting gallery and assessed her chances of winning the prizes on the top row. Pretty damn good. A cardboard box full of trophies and medals stashed in Jerry's basement attested to that—unless the guns were rigged. She didn't feel the Callaways were like that, though.

One of the older women, lean with streaks of gray in her short chestnut hair, was sitting in a camp chair outside the Big Top, keeping an eye out for any members of the public that might jump the white picket fence to steal a glimpse of the rehearsals. She lowered her book, watching Tammy approach, and then a smile of recognition flashed.

Tessa, Tammy remembered: a long-time employee who operated one of the food stands, who had been thrilled beyond measure when Rollo had financed a smart new trailer. Tammy had worked with her on the color and layout.

"Tammy!" She pushed herself to her feet and came forward, giving Tammy a warm hug. "It's good to see you again."

"Hi, Tessa. How is life in the new trailer?"

"Wonderful. I love it. There's so much more room with the slide-outs. One or two things need attention, but Rollo says you'll fix up anything in no time." She gestured at the entrance to the enormous tent. "Are you here to take a peek at rehearsal? Our contortionists—Gaye and Marco, remember them?—are trying a new routine." She laughed. "Makes me ache just to watch them."

"Sure. You coming in?"

"No, I need to stay here; there's a band of pesky teenagers who keep jumping the fence. Hugo's around the back watching out there." She made a face. "Not happy about it either; thinks it's beneath him. Born lazy: there's a lot less to do now that everything's new. Before, there was always something to mend or fix."

"I'll catch up with you later, then." Tammy pushed through the Big Top's closed flap and perched on a chair in the front row of the premium seating.

Gaye, a small-framed girl of eighteen with a neat cap of ebony hair and dramatic deep brown eyes, spotted her and waved. She said something to her brother, and then Marco unfolded himself and waved too. Both were dressed in close-fitting black pants and t-shirts, with dark ankle socks.

"OK to watch?" called Tammy.

"Sure!" Gaye gave her a thumbs up, punched a few buttons on the boom box nearby, and as the strains of dramatic music filled the air, the two started again. They began with an exaggerated bow to their audience of one, and Tammy played up to them with enthusiastic hand clapping. Nearby, a couple of men testing the rigging stopped to watch.

Amazing, Tammy thought, watching the sinuous movements unfold as Gaye and Marco flowed from one artfully balanced pose to another, interspersing them by prowling around each other like predatory cats. She held her breath when Gaye balanced on one hand on Marco's raised foot, seeing how they kept their weight evenly distributed as they moved. How long would it take to be that good? How many hours of rehearsal, how many falls?

Someone slipped into the seat beside her. "Good, aren't they?"

Tammy glanced briefly to see who it was. One of the road crew, wearing a dark t-shirt and tight jeans. He had a pack of cigarettes rolled into the sleeve of his t-shirt and a gold chain around his neck. He grinned at her, his eyes black, piercing, and confident, and sat back with his arms spread along the backs of each adjoining seat.

One of which was hers.

Big, muscled, and over-confident. Ladies' man. More accurately, she thought, a wannabe ladies' man.

"Wonderful," she said. "Mesmerizing. Excuse me." She gave him a brief smile and turned back to the contortionists. "I don't want to miss a thing."

"They look even better in costume," he said. "If you're staying a few days, you'll see the act tomorrow night." There was a questioning lilt in his voice.

"We'll be here." Tammy sat forward a little, propping her chin in both hands with her elbows resting on her knees. Twenty feet away from them, Gaye's body unwound itself like rubber, moving effortlessly into a pose that saw both feet planted firmly beside her head before she slid into the next pose.

"You're with that RV place, aren't you? Where Rollo bought all the fancy new trailers and motorhomes."

"Uh-huh."

"I'm Hugo."

"I'm Tammy," she said reluctantly. Instinctively, she didn't much care for the man, but for the sake of the Callaways, she would be polite - and because Tammy Dyson had been raised to be polite unless she had good reason not to be.

Hugo. The name sounded familiar, and then she remembered why. She spared him a glance. "Are you the one helping Tessa to shoo away the kids trying to get a sneak peek?"

"I've just come in. There's nobody out there," he said, his voice defensive. "And so what if a couple of kids spy on some rehearsals? What they see is nothing like the real show."

Tammy returned her gaze to Gaye and Marco, now changing the tempo and doing rapid backflips and other movements she couldn't give a name to. "I imagine it's a security thing," she said neutrally. "And insurance, if they get into something they shouldn't and injure themselves."

"Yeah, well—"

He never got to finish his sentence because an annoyed bellow sounded from across the other side of the tent, where another member of the crew stood holding a guilty-looking teenage boy in a firm grip. *"Hugo!"*

Hugo leaped to his feet with a muttered expletive, vaulted the low perimeter that formed the ring, and hurried across, forcing Marco to abort a move when he barged through their rehearsal space.

"Damn it!" Tammy heard him call out as he neared the other man. "I checked out the back not five minutes ago. I—"

Marco flung up his hands and scowled. Gaye rolled her eyes and shook her head.

There was always one, thought Tammy. One who thought he was above following instructions; who thought brawn was more important than brains. She had a finely honed instinct for men like Hugo. If he had decided she would make a tempting candidate for his charms, he'd be haunting her at every opportunity.

A carefully calculated putdown would do it, but she had already seen that Hugo didn't like being told.

Stay polite; she reminded herself. It was only for a week.

With a thumbs-up and a few warm words of praise to Gaye and Marco, she slipped away while Hugo was still spouting excuses.

CHAPTER 4

Time to Tell Rollo

"Much as I love my little gypsy house on wheels," Georgie said, "It is nice to have somewhere this big to hold meetings." She wriggled into a corner of Jerry's wickedly comfortable leather sofa in the slide-out section of his motorhome and swung her feet up onto Scott's knees. Trixxi sat on her haunches, looked up mournfully, and whined.

Scott leaned down, scooped up the poodle, and deposited her on Georgie's lap. "There you go," he said to Trixxi. "As an official mascot, you deserve to be treated right."

Tammy, sitting at the cafe lounge with a glass of soda in front of her, made kissy noises at Trixxi. "The only good thing Jaxx Saxby did for us was let us have her dog," she commented. "I bet she doesn't miss her. Too busy hosting her *Unsolved Mysteries* and pretending to be a hot-shot crime investigator." She shot a look across the table at Jerry. "Does she ever mention Trix?"

Georgie was amused to see Jerry shift uncomfortably in his seat. Jaxx was still maintaining an unrelenting campaign to steal the eminently eligible heir to the Johnny B. Goode RV Empire away from his "upstart wannabe girlfriend", as she had been heard to call Tammy. Rarely did a day pass without Jerry receiving a phone call, text message, email, or video call. He had moved on from being flattered to adopting a hunted expression whenever he heard her name.

Tammy reached over and patted him sympathetically on the hand. "You can answer. I know you and Jaxx talk every day, darling."

"It's not my fault. I swear it." He looked around the room as though expecting Jaxx to pop out of a cupboard. "What can I do? After her program aired, we were swamped with orders. She tells *everyone* about our Platinum Customer Care, yadda yadda yadda. If I refuse her calls now, she'll get mad and tweet it within five minutes."

"I know." Tammy put her head on one side with a pretty frown. "And gosh, now it's been, what, three weeks since the last personal visit to fix a leaky faucet or whatever? Must be just about time to go to her rescue again."

He put his head in his hands. "Tammy. Don't."

Much as she enjoyed seeing her brother paying for years of treating other girlfriends like playthings, Georgie judged that it was time to break in. He wasn't, after all, the only one being bombarded with her calls. "She phones me every other day too. She won't take no for an answer, so I've given in. I—"

Tammy gasped. "You've given in? Georgie, no. You're *not* going to do that psychic show with her!"

"No, no. Never that." Widening her eyes in horror, Georgie made flapping motions. "But I finally caved and agreed to do a fifteen-minute reading now and then on whatever case she's investigating. And," she said with satisfaction, "I charge her an arm and a leg for it. She's the one client who *deserves* exorbitant rates."

"Because you're solving her cases for her," Scott pointed out. He looked at the others. "Have you seen the show? The first two episodes have aired. She's got Georgie on the credits as her Secret Psychic."

Startled, Georgie looked at him. "*Has* she?"

"Well, sort of. It must be you," Scott said. "You're the only psychic she's consulting, and she said she could never reveal who it is because you're her secret weapon against fighting crime, and she doesn't want you to be a target."

"She actually *says* that?"

"In the introduction to each show. Yes."

An image of a blackened frame and ashes, all that had remained of her gypsy trailer after Jaxx's stalker had set fire to it, flashed through Georgie's mind. That had given her more than enough of a taste of being a target.

Trust Jaxx to put the idea in people's minds.

"Dammit," she said crossly, feeling her temper rise. "Jaxx hasn't got the sense she was born with. I'm going to *triple* my fee."

Jerry, relieved to have the focus taken off him, seized the moment. "Let's forget Jaxx for the moment. Right now, we need Georgie the Secret Psychic more than she does."

Georgie blinked. "Jerry, I'm flattered. But what's going on? I was going to grab a minute to talk to all of you, but you called me over here first." She nodded at Scott. "All I got from him was '…wait until everyone is together.'"

"Sabotage," Jerry said succinctly. "Those teething problems we were supposed to fix? Not our fault. Not unless a pump can attack itself with a wrench. Or a brand new hose can slit itself with a knife."

Georgie's heart gave a huge thump. She hadn't been wrong, then. Something nasty was going on behind the scenes at the Callaway Circus.

"We've got a few more little problems to check out tomorrow," Scott told her, reaching over to pat Trixxi and then squeezing Georgie's hand. "I wouldn't be surprised to find it's more than teething problems there, too."

"It fits." Adjusting the cushion behind her, Georgie sat upright a little more. "Now for my news: I saw it too. When Ginger came by today."

"Ginger came?" Tammy's eyebrows flew up. "I thought she was dead against fortune-telling."

"She's dead against *being* a fortune-teller; I don't think she's got anything against it per se." Georgie ran through her session with Ginger as closely as she could remember it, finishing with her feeling that someone in the circus camp meant harm to others. "I have no idea who. I *did* have an uncomfortable feeling about the new acts, Angelique and Travis—but I don't know if it's because of this or just because they're out for what they can get. They struck me as being a bit calculating."

"And Ginger didn't pick up on any of this?" Jerry asked, frowning.

"No, all she could think about was having meatloaf for dinner." Georgie laughed wryly. "The Callaways can rule her out as a fortune-teller. She'd be exposed as a fraud in the first hour."

"All that money on a gorgeous new gypsy trailer," Tammy said mournfully, "and they can't even use it." She thought for a moment. "It's bright and colorful. They could turn it into a booth, sell crystal balls and tarot cards and stuff from it. Scarves, clothes…"

"Forget marketing, Tams. The gypsy wagon is the least of our worries," Georgie said. "What worries me is that Ginger herself might have been a victim. She put her accident down to equipment failure, but…" she shrugged. "I don't know. Something doesn't feel right."

"It's more than a feeling," Scott pointed out. "There's direct evidence of tampering. We have to tell Rollo."

Georgie agreed with him on that one. They didn't have much choice, really, but to tell him that the problems with Cassandra's motorhome were more than just minor maintenance problems. And Rollo, she felt instinctively, would have enough sense—and self-control—to work out the best way to handle this.

Police? Maybe…or maybe they'd do better to give the culprit enough rope to hang himself.

Or herself.

"I think we can safely assume it's not Ginger," she said, thinking it through. "She certainly didn't set herself up for a serious accident. Cassandra? I doubt it—what's her motive? She's already the apple of her father's eye for her aerial skills, and her motorhome was damaged."

"Don't rule people out because of that, though," Jerry said immediately. "Whoever it is could damage their own property easily enough to throw people off the scent. I've done it myself."

All eyes swung toward Jerry.

"When?" demanded Georgie.

"Several times," he said, grinning. "When we were kids. You got the blame a few times. Sorry about that."

Georgie thought back, her brow furrowing in concentration. "My dollhouse. Your gas station. That was you all the time."

"Yup." Feeling the others' eyes on him, he explained. "I accidentally damaged Georgie's new dollhouse. I wanted some of the removable panels to use for my wooden gas station. Unfortunately, they didn't come out easily."

"You broke them." Georgie was indignant all over again, remembering her grief. "On the day of my birthday party. It was brand new, and you did it. I *knew* you did it. I saw you come out of my room."

"And while you were running to Mom," he said, "I snapped out some of the walls of my gas station and then followed you. Also wailing."

"And blaming me. *Me.*"

"It worked," he said. "I knew Mom wouldn't think it was you. She ended up believing it was one of the kids at the party. Her money was on the Gleason boy, although she couldn't come out and accuse him outright."

"You let him take the rap!" Georgie shook her head. "You were such a little creep."

"I was," he admitted. "But I'm a reformed character." He sent Tammy a full-wattage super-charming Jerry smile. "Ever since I met Tammy."

"Not reformed enough," Tammy said coolly. "Long way to go, Jer."

A quick flash of frustration showed in Jerry's eyes, gone in an instant but still there. At least, Georgie thought it was frustration. It could have been hurt, too, but she was still steamed about the dollhouse, so she put that aside.

He'd get Tammy's complete devotion when he earned it, and not a second before.

"Anyway…" he returned to the subject. "My point is, don't exclude anyone because they *appear* to be a victim. Those of us who have spent half a lifetime perfecting the con know better."

"All right. We don't rule out Cassandra." Georgie was prepared to give way on that one, although her instincts said Cassandra was OK. "Going just on my instincts, intuition, whatever—information from the crystal ball—I'd take another look at those two who haven't been here long, Angelique and Travis. As for the others, I'll have to poke around a bit more."

"Add Hugo to the list," Tammy put in. "One of the general hands with too much testosterone and gold chains around his neck. He was supposed to be watching the perimeter this afternoon but left his post to come and chat me up."

Jerry looked at her keenly. "Want me to scare him off?"

"Nope. I can do that myself, if necessary." Tammy drummed her nails on the table, eyeing him. "I mean it, Jerry. Let me handle it."

"Sure." Jerry's voice sounded a trifle clipped, although his face remained good-humored. "Anyone else?"

They all looked at each other and shrugged. One day wasn't enough to tell.

"Right, then." Scott decided for all of them. "Tomorrow, after Jerry and I check out the rest of the fix-it list from Rollo, we'll know if anyone else has been a victim. Jerry, as the representative of the RV Empire, you can break the news."

"I'll check out the crystal ball again in the morning," Georgie decided. "And get Ginger to show me around, get more of a sense of everyone's role here. Now we're pretty sure there's a traitor in the camp; I can slip in a few questions. Like who has been working here for a long time, who's a recent hire."

"And any family tensions—or disagreements between the crew," Tammy said. "Tessa didn't seem too keen on Hugo this afternoon."

Trixxi squirmed on Georgie's lap, which reminded her of Jaxx, and that in turn reminded her of Layla, who was spending a week with one of Jaxx's cameramen on the east coast while the rest of them were with the circus. It just didn't seem right to be embarking on another Crystal Ball Team Investigation without Layla.

"Layla's going to be annoyed at missing this," she said, mainly to Tammy. The two of them had been inseparable for more than a year.

"I call her most days. She can be our long-distance consultant." Tammy grinned. "If she can tear herself away from Seth."

They all laughed. They were all a bit surprised that Layla's relationship with Seth was working at all, considering they were both on the road most of the time—and rarely in the same place.

"Layla's a whiz with the computer," Tammy pointed out. "While she's waiting for Seth to stop filming, or downloading, or editing or whatever else he has to do, she can be looking stuff up for us."

"True." Georgie lifted Trixxi off her lap and handed her to Scott so she could get up. "I'm whacked. I'm off to bed, ready to poke around tomorrow."

She just hoped she wasn't going to be poking somewhere that unleashed something dark and dangerous.

CHAPTER 5

A Surprise Visitor

'Something dark and dangerous' turned up at her door unexpectedly the following day, shortly after Scott had left to do the rounds with Jerry. Georgie opened the door to find herself face to face with a swarthy giant with thick black eyebrows, a bushy beard, and an unnerving direct stare out of deep brown eyes. The only reason they were face to face was that he was standing on the bottom step.

Hagrid, was her first reaction, as a shiver went down her back. But the Hagrid in the Harry Potter stories was one of the good guys. This one, she wasn't so sure about.

"Hello," he rumbled, nodding at her without smiling. "You're the gypsy fortune-teller."

"Uh, yes." Flustered, Georgie tried to push

away her natural fear of someone so huge just inches from her nose. "I'm not actually so much a gypsy. My great-grandmother was." Gathering her wits, she took a deep breath. "Can I help you?"

"I'd like to see it. Your crystal ball." His voice sounded like rocks tumbling together in a spin dryer. "If that's all right."

It was the 'if that's all right', tacked on the end, that made her release her grip on the doorframe and breathe again. He was a giant, she told herself; therefore, he probably had something to do with the circus, and therefore he had a right to see her. She supposed.

She stepped back, flicking a wary glance over him. Most of her bigger clients found the bench seat at the table a bit tight. "It might be a bit cramped for you, ah… sorry, what's your name?"

"Zachary."

"Would you be more comfortable in a chair?"

He laughed, and the rumble made the whole trailer vibrate. "Broken a lot of chairs in my time. I usually sit on the bed."

Rattled, Georgie stepped aside to let him past. A man the size of a house was going to sit on her bed while he looked at her crystal ball.

She wasn't even sure whether there was enough oxygen in the small space for the two of them.

"I'll get a chair anyway," she said. "So I can sit near you."

By the time she fetched a chair from outside and brought it in, he had already taken her crystal ball from the shelf and was sitting on the bed with it in his hands. It was dwarfed by his huge palms.

Frowning, Georgie opened her mouth to object but shut it again when she saw the expression on his face. He was gazing intently at it, but there was an odd look in his eyes, as though he wasn't in the room with her but staring through layers of meaning, focusing on something only he could see.

Quietly, Georgie sat on the chair in front of him and waited, studying his face while her heartbeat settled down. Something in her memory clicked: an image floated into her mind of Zachary in the background the day before, when Rollo had conducted their introductory tour. He had been in the Big Top, half-underneath a small stage area, working with another crew member on some lighting and sound equipment. All she had seen were boots and an arm and a flash of a bearded face.

Handy with tools…and Scott had said they were looking at sabotage.

She dismissed the thought instantly. No, not this guy.

Suddenly, he was back in the real world, raising his head to look at her.

"Your crystal ball needs moonlight, earth. Natural revitalization. It wouldn't hurt to bury it for a few nights. A week's better."

Open-mouthed, she stared at him.

Gently, he set her crystal ball beside him on the bed and delved into a deep pocket in his loose-fitting cargo pants. "Look."

She watched while he extracted an object rolled up in a layer of crimson silk and then unwrapped it.

It was another crystal ball. Smaller than hers and a lot brighter. Georgie's eyes flicked between the two crystals. She hadn't imagined it: her crystal ball *was* looking dull.

Her great-grandma Rosa had never said a word about exposing the crystal ball to moonlight, much less bury it. Although, she thought, wrinkling her forehead in concentration, she could vaguely remember reading something about it when she first owned it—when she was desperate to find out how it all worked. But then, things had taken off so quickly she hadn't followed up on it.

She finally found her voice. "Is that what you do with yours?"

"Yes." He held it out to her, cupped in one hand

with the other resting beneath it, as though passing over something precious. "Want to see?"

"You don't mind?"

"Some people don't like others to touch their crystal balls," he said in his strange, harsh voice. "I allow some, not all. Like you." He nodded at her crystal ball, still resting beside him. "You ask some people to put hands on it when you're doing a reading."

How did he know that? Unsettled, Georgie reached out and took his crystal ball, instinctively using both hands as Zachary had. Her fingers brushed his, and she felt the humming energy instantly, both from the crystal ball and the man.

He was like a generator, charged with heat and a strange force. She had a moment's impression of a deep, dark well, filled with heat and potential.

Zachary nodded as though satisfied about something. He sat back, crossed his arms, and watched her.

For pity's sake. Who *was* this man?

Tearing her gaze away from the bottomless wells of his dark eyes, she glanced down at the glinting ball in her hands. It felt pure and happy.

Happy? Where had that come from?

Without thinking twice, she placed it in her lap

and held out her hands for her own. "Can you pass me mine, please?"

Zachary did so after first smoothing his hands over the surface in a brief caress.

Georgie sat with the two crystal balls side by side, watching the light refract from Zachary's, splitting into bright shards, while her crystal ball seemed to wrap itself around the quickly forming mist in its interior. Hers was dull in comparison to Zachary's, but the two of them together raised the temperature of the air around her.

A shiver, delicious yet somehow scary, ran up her spine.

There was more energy in the air than she'd ever felt before—but oddly, it was as though the two crystal balls were keeping their secrets—unless it was all going to Zachary.

She glanced up at him and wasn't surprised to see him watching her closely.

"I can feel the buzz. Loud and clear. What I'm *not* getting is any sort of message." She arched a brow in inquiry. "Are you?"

He drew in a deep breath, not breaking his gaze, and shook his head. "No. And I haven't been getting anything since you arrived." His dark eyes grew speculative. "I was wondering if it was some action you'd taken."

"I've done nothing."

"Then it must be the way they interact." His words in themselves were inoffensive, but the gravelly rumble of his voice made him sound aggressive. "Tonight, let your crystal bathe in the moonlight."

"Zachary." She thought about the best way to put what she wanted to know and decided that a direct approach would work best with him. "I can sense that you know what you're doing. I can feel the power." She drummed up a weak smile. "It's a bit scary. But if you're a fortune-teller—if you have The Sight—then why on earth is Theodora trying to force Ginger into the role? Why not you?"

He reached over and plucked his crystal ball from her lap, and for a moment, Georgie felt a keen disappointment. Watching it being wrapped in crimson silk and stowed back in the depths of his pocket, she felt as though she was losing part of herself.

Ridiculous.

He hadn't answered her question, so she repeated it. "Why aren't you the Callaway Circus fortune-teller?"

"Probably," he said, "because nobody but you knows about it. And I would prefer you didn't tell them."

This was getting weirder and weirder. "I won't, of course… but why not?"

"I'm here because of Ginger." He stood up, and the whole trailer rocked. "I saw a news item on her the day she fell. People in the audience were filming her with their phones, and the evening news was filled with clips from different angles. I knew right away it wasn't an accident."

Georgie stood up, too, rather than stare up at him. He stood with his head bent, so he didn't bang it on the ceiling. "What did you see?"

He dismissed that with a wave of his hand. "Nothing. Nothing on the video clips and the investigators and insurance people have been all over it, too. I just knew in the same way that *you* would know. I had to come. Talked my way into a job." He gestured at her sink. "OK if I get a drink of water?"

"I've got some cold." She went to the fridge and extracted a corked bottle of water, then poured him a glass.

Zachary drank it, staring out through the colored panes of glass in the door to the action in the circus grounds beyond. "What brought you here? Were you called, like me?"

"Theoretically, I'm here to give Ginger a few tips on fortune-telling so that she can do it as one of the attractions. She made a quick decision to tell him all she knew. "I met with her yesterday, enough for me to know that she hasn't got a hope of doing this. She'd hate it, and the customers would pick her as a fraud in five minutes. Less, perhaps."

He leaned a hip against the small kitchen counter. "You said 'theoretically'."

"I did come here because they asked me to train Ginger in crystal-ball reading. But this has happened before: like you, I seem to be drawn toward people who need me." She hesitated, thinking that she should consult with the others in the CBI team first, but took the plunge. "My brother and my partner found evidence of sabotage yesterday when they checked the RVs. And when I did the reading with Ginger, I picked up something else. There's evil in the Callaway Circus. Someone here is working against them. As yet, I don't know who."

He grunted, his eyes looking past her shoulder while he thought. "Ginger's accident was months ago. So why now?"

"I don't know."

"And neither of us can do a reading because our crystal balls are fighting each other. Or canceling each other out. Something like that."

"It seems that way."

Zachary put the glass down and pointed at her crystal ball, now resting on the table. "Don't forget: put that out tonight. It's a full moon. We'll see if it makes any difference to a reading tomorrow. Meanwhile, I'll keep an eye on Ginger and the other performers."

"Wait," Georgie said, stopping him as he put one massive paw on the doorknob, ready to head off. "You've been here for months now, right?"

"Ten weeks."

"You'd know the performers and the crew well. Any suspicions?"

"Some," he said. "But no proof. Otherwise, I would have taken action."

"Are you prepared to share the names?"

"Not at the moment." His eyes were intelligent. "You seem to be the real deal, but just in case, we'll see what you discover tomorrow. Meanwhile, take care."

With that, he was gone.

Take care, she thought. Yes, she'd do that all right.

But what she needed was a nice big fat clue.

Moonlight, huh? All right, if that's what it took. Tonight, her crystal ball was going to bathe in the cool night air and crisp white moonlight.

But would it lead her to the saboteur?

CHAPTER 6

Poleaxed

The following day, after Scott had gone off to find Jerry and check out the rest of the RVs, Georgie lifted her crystal ball down from the roof of her gypsy trailer, where it had spent the night under the moon. She looked at it critically. Was it marginally brighter after spending the night caressed by moonbeams?

Not so that you'd notice, she decided, but perhaps it needed more than one evening. On impulse, she carved a small hole into the earth beneath her trailer, tucked the crystal ball inside, and covered it with rich soil.

Nurtured by moonlight and earth. She had no idea why, but she trusted Zachary.

Time to find out a bit more about the employees of the Callaway circus. Georgie went to look for Ginger and found her inside the Big Top with three girls between eight and ten years old, watching with a critical eye while they went over and over basic tumbling movements on mats and a balance beam. With her was a member of the crew, a dark-haired man with a stocky, compact body. He walked beside a girl with honey blonde hair caught up in a perky ponytail as she carefully placed one foot in front of the other on a wire suspended about three feet from the ground, using a pole to help keep balance.

"That's it. Nice work, Tawnya," he was saying, his voice light and cheerful. "Don't hesitate. Keep moving, nice and confident, and use the pole to stay steady."

Ginger spotted Georgie and held up five fingers before pointing at her watch.

Georgie stayed in the background and watched. She didn't know much about gymnastics or balancing, but the kids seemed to be good to her. A girl with short dark hair jumped up on a four-inch-wide balance beam, only six inches or so from the ground, and ran lightly along it and then back again before somersaulting into the air and coming down again, both feet landing safely on the beam. Beside her, Ginger was alert, ready to grab her if she miscued. The girl rocked precariously, her arms windmilling, her toes curling around the beam, and then steadied. She turned to Ginger with a wide, toothy smile. "Third time in a row!"

"Top job, Candy. Now see if you can nail the dismount."

"Easy." Aware that she had an audience, she bowed and then somersaulted off the beam, grinning first at Ginger and then at Georgie.

"Well done." Ginger checked her watch. "Good session, kids. Now it's time for school. Off you go."

They all groaned in unison. "Just a bit longer?" wheedled Candy.

"We'll run through it again after school. Be here at two-thirty." Ginger looked at the man with her, who was shifting the mats over to a corner out of the way. "That suit you, Doyle?"

"Yep. I need to give Hugo a hand with a few things after lunch, but I should be clear by then." He nodded at Georgie, a smile lighting his eyes. "I'm Doyle Arrowsmith. I saw you coming in yesterday with the others."

"Hi, Doyle. I'm Georgie, in the gypsy wagon." She shook hands. "I was watching you and Ginger with the kids. They seem to be really good."

"They are." Doyle got on one end of the beam while Ginger took the other, and they moved it over with the mats. "Ginger's the one with the expertise, though. I just help out with safety."

"You're underselling yourself," Ginger told him. "You know exactly what to tell them to help them get it right." To Georgie, she said: "I'm the helper here. Doyle's been teaching the kids for months. He's one of our all-rounders. The audience loves him; he plays a clown for the show, joining in most acts as comic relief. But you can't do that unless you've been a tumbler yourself."

"A failed tumbler," Doyle said with mock sadness. "Never really good enough to do the difficult routines. So I clown around and help train the next generation." He cast aside the sad face and grinned at Georgie. "Works for me. So, what's it like being a fortune-teller? Are you for real, or is it all about reading people?" Quickly, seeming to realize that his words might offend, he added, "I don't mean to be rude. I just don't know how it works."

"I guess you'd say I'm for real," Georgie said, smiling back. "But having said that, I can't always guarantee results—and sometimes I can't see a thing, unfortunately. That's when I *do* try to read people, see if I can pick something up. I've often wished I could read minds. Don't worry; your secrets are safe from me."

He laughed. "I might have a dark side, for all

you know. Aren't some people scared of clowns? A red nose and a painted grin could hide all kinds of things."

"Oh, you." Ginger gave him a cheerful shove. "Take your murky depths off to clown practice. Georgie and I can have coffee and talk about how I can convince Mom I'm not a fortune-teller."

He winked and strode off, whistling.

"He's great with the kids," Ginger said, watching him. "That's what I'd like to do, you know, just work with the kids, coaching them. I was always too busy before, but now my Lucy wants to start…" Her eyes clouded, and Georgie knew that she was thinking of the accident. "I want to make sure she does it right."

"Why *couldn't* you work with the kids? Wouldn't that be ideal? Somebody has to train them."

"It's Doyle's job. That and his clown routines. I don't want to take it away from him. I usually come over to lend a hand, but it was his gig before I stopped doing aerial work."

Hmm. Georgie just nodded but tucked away the information for later. Ginger, coaching the next talented band of tumblers and aerialists. It *felt* right.

All they needed to do was talk Theodora out of this gypsy fortune-teller idea.

But first, coffee with Ginger…and a decision about whether to tell her of her suspicions about the accident.

It was a scary thing to know that someone wouldn't stop at causing an accident—or even death.

After he left Georgie that morning, Scott picked up Jerry, and the two of them spent most of the day checking out not only the fix-it list that Rollo handed them but every motorhome and trailer that had come from the Johnny B. Goode RV Empire. Most items on the list were simple fixes: loose screws, a sticky catch, a slightly misaligned window screen. Cassandra's motorhome had the most blatant sabotage, but they also found loose wheel nuts on Rollo's motorhome. Not just on one wheel, but on three.

"Bloody hell," Jerry said, his face grim. "They meant business. I've seen the aftermath of accidents with loose wheel nuts. Too loose or too tight, they can shear off. Lose a wheel at the wrong time…and it's not a roadside fix if the wheel nuts break off. It has to go up on a hoist."

"At least if they know what's going on, they can

keep watch, I suppose." Scott put away the last of his tools. "We might as well break the news now as later. Think they'll be calling in the police?"

"Maybe…maybe not. They've got a show on tonight, and they won't want to disrupt it." Jerry sighed. "It's just after three now…we've got, what, four hours before the show begins? This is the last thing they'll want to hear from us."

He was right. Rollo, predictably, looked poleaxed.

"*Sabotage?*" He stared at Jerry in disbelief before sinking onto a chair at the dining table; his customary exuberance abruptly dimmed.

"I'm afraid so." Briefly, Jerry outlined what he and Scott had found that morning and in Cassandra's motorhome the night before. "We checked every one of the units that came from us; fixed all the minor stuff for you—but after seeing Cassandra's, we also ran through our own checklist. Wheels, tires, motor, hoses, fittings—as much as we could under the circumstances. For a thorough check, you'd have to take the whole lot back to the factory at Elkhart, though."

The expression on Rollo's face made it clear what he thought of that idea.

"I know," Jerry said. "You have a circus to run. You can't cancel everything to do that."

Rollo sucked in a deep breath. "You got that right. And it'd be on my dollar, too, because sabotage isn't covered by any guarantee." Without looking at Theodora, he held up a hand to stop her. "I know what you're going to say, Teddy: we have insurance, besides having plenty of money in the bank, and safety is paramount, all of that. I'm not arguing with you there. But there are other things to think about—the negative publicity if this gets out not being the least of it."

"I wasn't going to say that at all," Theodora said indignantly, refusing to be silenced. She threw both hands out wide. "I know we can pay. But I'm *furious*. FURIOUS! How dare someone do this to us. One of our *own!*"

"You don't know that," Rollo pointed out, a nerve twitching in his neck. "It could be someone from outside."

"But not likely," Scott said. "You have a security guard at night, and during the day, everyone's keeping an eye open for fence-hoppers."

"Let me think." Rollo rubbed his knuckles across his forehead. "Let me think, what to do…"

There was a knock at the door.

"Whoever it is, get rid of them," Rollo said irritably.

Theodora stomped to the door and threw it open. "Sorry, it's not—oh, it's you, Ginger."

"We saw Scott's truck here," came Ginger's voice. "So Georgie and I thought—"

"It's not really the best time right now," Theodora cut her off. "Can this wait?"

Outside, Georgie spoke up. "Theodora, this isn't about Ginger and fortune-telling. There's something else you need to know."

Hearing the tension in her voice, Scott stood up. Georgie had already told him about Zachary's visit and suspicions, so he had a fair idea of what it was about. He walked over and put a hand on Theodora's shoulder. "Teddy—"

"*Theodora*," she snapped.

"Theodora," he said soothingly. "Theodora, Georgie knows about this. And I think she has something else to tell you."

Georgie nodded at him gratefully, but Ginger didn't wait. "Mom, we're coming in." She gave Theodora no choice but to move aside, and the moment the door had closed behind her, took her mother by both arms. Her face was white and pinched, and the freckles across her cheeks stood out. "Mom, my accident…it…" Her voice cracked. "Oh, Mom, maybe it *wasn't* an accident."

CHAPTER 7

Roll Up! Roll Up!

In the Big Top that night, Georgie sat next to Scott, thinking how much she liked the feeling of his large, warm hand wrapped around hers. Comforting. She squeezed his fingers and felt the answering pressure. She glanced at him and found him looking at her questioningly. Georgie smiled and nestled closer. An intuitive man, he would know that she was concerned for the Callaways, anxious to find the enemy within the ranks before they did any more damage—and glad that Scott was with her to investigate.

Messages without words, she thought; affection communicated by a grip, a squeeze, a meeting of the eyes.

That was what poor Ginger needed right now; someone of her own to be with her, hold her.

Someone who would watch her back. Of course, her family would do that—Rollo had called in his other three children to tell them what was going on —but still.

"I hope Rollo doesn't regret his decision to leave the police out of it," she said in an undertone, conscious of the people in the row behind them. It was only five minutes or so until showtime, and most of the audience had already taken their seats.

"No proof," Scott murmured. "Ginger's accident was months ago, and they all put it down to equipment failure."

"Which it was, technically."

"Equipment failure cleverly engineered by someone."

"He might have left fingerprints in Cassandra's motorhome."

"He or she," Scott corrected her. "Possibly. I'm betting not."

Georgie gazed up at the aerial silk and the high wire, up in the gloomy heights of the Big Top, waiting for the performers. It was a long way to fall.

As Ginger knew first hand.

But tonight, Rollo had checked and re-checked the scaffolding and every part of the mechanism that would keep his performers safe. He laughed and joked as he did so, stopping for a chat with this person and that, so the saboteur wouldn't guess that he'd been rumbled. The broken water pump could have been put down to damage from rocks thrown up on country roads; the split hoses to faulty stock. Loose wheel nuts could be attributed to a mechanic becoming distracted at the wrong time. But everything taken together? No.

And *certainly* not on a million-dollar motorhome recently delivered from Jerry B. Goode's RV Empire. Jerry was taking it as a personal affront.

Georgie shaded her eyes against the lights, peering across at the seats on the other side, where Tammy and Jerry were sitting with some of the town dignitaries. The mayor had spotted Jerry, recognized him from the TV ads, and insisted that they sit with him. He was in the market for a motorhome—and no doubt anticipating a deal on the price.

The cheerful background music faded away, and the lights dimmed. There was a rustle of expectation in the crowd and enthusiastic applause.

Everyone loved a circus.

A single spotlight flared and pinpointed a plain black box, right in the center of the ring. The music swelled, building the drama, until the lid of the box slowly opened, showing a pair of steepled hands glowing an unearthly silver. They writhed and snaked in the air, performing a sinuous dance, and then a body in a glittering silver suit rose and flowed out of the box, undulating like a serpent.

Given the close-fitting hood and silver mask, it was impossible to tell who it was, but after doing the rounds earlier in the day, Georgie knew she was looking at Gaye. Right on cue, Marco slid in from outside the spotlight, circling Gaye in his matching silver suit.

They mimicked two silver serpents, hissing and attacking, weaving their limbs into impossible positions while they swayed to the music. Then twin ropes of golden silk were lowered, and the crowd was mesmerized for the next ten minutes, gasping and cheering when the two continued their dance in the air.

At one point, Gaye plummeted toward the ground, and the crowd shrieked. Georgie jumped to her feet, her heart thudding, only to have Scott tug her down beside him again. "Part of the act," he said, as Gaye came to shuddering halt inches from the end of the ribbon of silk, followed by Marco performing the same maneuver.

"Oh my goodness." Georgie slumped beside him, her pulse still racing. "I don't think I can stand too much of this." All she could think of was

Ginger, slipping from the same height but with nothing to break her fall.

Scott leaned over and kissed her cheek. "It's okay. Just enjoy the show."

And, for the next two hours, Georgie was mostly able to shut down the panic button and do just that.

But she couldn't turn her mind off.

Zachary. For some reason, his name kept playing in her mind.

Tomorrow, she'd pay him a visit.

She couldn't help breathing a sigh of relief when the show ended without any casualties, gathering with the others to congratulate the performers. That took some time because so many of the towns-folk wanted autographed photos and videos of the show's stars. Callaway's Circus was well and truly on the map, partly because of the enormous swell of publicity following the lottery win and the subse-quent revitalization of a circus that had been around for over a century. Decades before, Rollo Callaway had correctly predicted the swing away from performing animals and focused on tumbling, aerial work, and clever skits with talented clowns.

Now he was set to enjoy the fruit of years of labor —as long as the saboteur didn't break his spirit.

Georgie watched Rollo and Theodora effortlessly mixing with people of all ages and levels of society: local politicians, A-listers, humble families that just wanted to come up and say thanks and how much they had enjoyed the show.

She liked them, she realized. Larger-than-life Theodora, ebullient Rollo, all of their children. They deserved their success.

"Hey there." Doyle appeared at her elbow, still made up in clown paint and wearing garish clothes, right down to the exaggerated big shoes. "Enjoy the show?"

"It was fantastic. I had a minor heart attack or two watching the aerial show and the high-wire artists, but I survived." She gave him a friendly poke in the arm. "I see what Ginger means about you being an all-rounder. It can't be easy, blending into some of those tumbling routines the way you do." She glanced down at his feet and laughed. "Especially with shoes like that."

"My secret weapon. If I mess up, it looks like I'm supposed to be a klutz—isn't that what clowns do?" He leaned around her to introduce himself to Scott. "Hi. I'm Doyle. Clown and Jack-of-all-Trades. You're here with Jerry to fix the glitches?"

"More or less," Scott said. "I came with Georgie, but I'm a kind of general handyman."

A general handyman with a degree in environmental science, Georgie thought in amusement. To Scott, his degree was just a means to an end. He loved the outdoors, loved being a park ranger, loved working with his hands. A piece of paper mattered little.

Doyle nodded. "My trailer's isn't one of yours. It's only a couple of years old—well made, no problems. Didn't need a new one."

"We're happy to look it over for you anyway," Scott said. "Professional courtesy because Rollo placed such a big order. We're doing that for a few of the workers here that didn't have trailers or motorhomes replaced."

Georgie stole a look at him. He and Jerry had spent some time discussing how they might gain access to every RV in the circus without making it evident that something was wrong. The "professional courtesy" line seemed to work. Johnny B. Goode was known for superb after-sales service.

"Won't say no," Doyle said. "I can manage everyday repairs, replace a fuse—but I'm no mechanic."

"I'll check with Jerry, see who else is on the list, and then catch up with you to give you a time."

"Great." Doyle turned his head at a tug on his sleeve and grinned down at a couple of small children, nodding at their hovering parents. "Hey. Did you enjoy the show?"

"Yes," said the boy. He glanced at his parents, took a deep breath, and said, "I want to be a clown like you. Did you have to go to clown school?"

"No." Doyle squatted down to be on eye-level with the boy. "I just watched lots of clowns, at circuses and on Internet videos. And my dad was a clown." He looked up and grinned at the boy's parents. "But you know what? There are schools where kids can learn circus arts. Including being a clown."

"There are?" The parents exchanged a speculative glance.

"Yep, sure are. Some are in winter; some are in the summer break." Doyle reached into one of his bright patch pockets and pulled out a couple of brochures. "Here. You can read all about it." He handed it to the boy's mother.

Georgie watched while Doyle chatted to the two children for a bit longer and then waved goodbye, having them shrieking with laughter when he did a short series of cartwheels, big shoes and all.

"You're good with them," Georgie told him. "You mean there really is a circus school for kids?"

"Several of them. My dad works in one; that's why I have the brochures." He glanced away. "Hugo is looking impatient over there. I'd better help pack up. See you."

Georgie watched him walk away.

"I know that look," Scott said. "What's going through your mind?"

"I just had an idea. The Callaways take part of the year off, don't they? To recharge?"

"That's what I heard."

"I'm thinking of Ginger…she wants to settle down with Lucy, but she said she loves working with kids." Georgie shrugged. "I wonder if she's ever thought of starting up a Callaway Circus training school?" She looked over to where she could see Ginger's strawberry blonde head in a group around the circus children who had performed that night.

"A *training* school?" Scott looked incredulous. "That would cost a fortune to set up."

"The Callaways *have* a fortune."

"They still have a gypsy trailer empty, too, and waiting for their fortune teller. Are you going to fill that spot?"

"No, but…" Georgie's mind flew straight to Zachary. "But I can think of someone else who might."

CHAPTER 8

Staircase to Infinity

The next morning Georgie did what she always did, regardless of whether Rosa's crystal ball was being cooperative or not. She fished out her computer and spent an hour on the Internet, trolling for information. Rollo and Theodora could tell her plenty about the circus and its employees, but she wanted to get a handle on the public perception of the Callaway Circus.

She started with recent press releases about the revitalized circus and followed the trail back to its beginnings, decades in the past.

She was especially interested in Angelique and Travis, the most recent additions to the Callaway Flying Circus lineup. Their surname, she discovered, was Starr.

Starr. Georgie wrinkled her forehead in

thought. Starr... She knew that name. She clicked on the surname, which took her through to another page.

"Of course," she said out loud. The Americana All Starr Circus—she remembered seeing something about it on TV once, a show about the fate of old-fashioned circuses. It had been big, once.

Trixxi, hearing her voice, gave a half-hearted yip.

"The Americana All Starr Circus. There was a lot of publicity about cruelty to animals," she said, rubbing the top of Trixxi's head with her foot. She got a lazy lick in return. "Euuw, no licking...ah, here's more." Georgie scrolled down and clicked through to another page. "Oh, that's the connection. Solomon Starr was a small investor in the Callaway circus..." She continued to read. Solly Starr had been a daredevil aerialist as well as a good friend of Rollo's once. After Rollo bought out Solly's share, he and his wife Belinda left Callaway's and had taken over a couple of smaller circuses to form the bigger All Starr's. According to the gossip columns, there had been ongoing friction between Callaway's Circus and the Americana All Starrs.

Almost from the beginning, the Starr circus had steadily gone downhill. It continued to rely on animal acts as a big part of its lineup and had run foul of animal welfare groups. Hefty fines, negative publicity…the Starr circus continued to fade while Callaways held on to market share.

Now, Starr's was a fraction of its former size. It featured equestrian performances and second-rate tumbling and aerial work and just toured small towns in the country.

She searched for mention of Angelique and Travis Starr, Solly's son and daughter. Their Facebook pages yielded plenty of information: apparently, they had stayed with Starr's until Angelique snagged a stint with Cirque du Soleil. She hadn't lasted long…not quite good enough?

Soon after, the Callaways won the lottery and poured big dollars into refurbishment and new performers. It seemed that Angelique and her brother had made a beeline for money and fame, leaving their father in the lurch.

"Interesting," Georgie told Trixxi, bending down to pick her up and scratching her head while she watched a YouTube video. "Is that a motive, do you think, Trix? Solly Starr loses market share, while his former partner Rollo continues to do well? Then Solly's children decamp to the Callaways' smart new circus. The question is, are they here to build their careers or to do Solly's dirty work?"

Trixxi cocked her head on one side and looked at her, bright-eyed.

"You'd like to help, wouldn't you?" Georgie tapped her on the nose. "If you could only speak." She watched Angelique doing her Cirque du Soleil routine. "She's good. But what does she have to gain by sabotaging the Callaway circus? Unless Travis is the guilty one?"

She flicked back to an earlier tab that showed Travis at work. Accomplished, she thought, as many circus kids were who had grown up as performers - but she didn't think he was as good as Angelique.

If *he* was the saboteur, then why?

Might he be working with Angelique or against her? Both of them, or just one?

Or neither.

Who else would have the motive to destroy Rollo?

She sighed. "Getting nowhere here, Trixxi. I think I'll go and find Zachary. Be a good girl and wait here for me."

Trixxi whined, and Georgie could have sworn she gave a doggy frown.

"Don't want to get left behind? Oh, all right. You can come. But no getting under the tumbler's feet. If one of them falls on you, you'll be hamburger."

She shut down her laptop, and as an afterthought, slid her crystal ball into a shoulder bag. Maybe she should get a small one like Zachary's, which she could keep in her pocket.

Or just a pack of cards, like Scott. He didn't have to put *those* out in the moonlight or bury them so they could get revitalized.

She headed out to see what Zachary thought.

Some of the sideshows and booths were already open, getting ready for the influx of townspeople when the gates opened in a few hours' time. There would be plenty to do and see while they were waiting for the matinee performance to begin. Georgie walked past several of them, greeting the attendants who were restocking shelves or checking their equipment. She quickened her step as she went past the Wild West Shootout, where one of the ground crew, wearing a tight t-shirt and snug jeans, was standing around talking to Bob, the gray-haired man who operated the booth.

Bob nodded back at her, and the crew member straightened up and smoothed a hand over his hair. He called to her, waving at the prizes lined up on the shelves. "Hey, Georgie! Come and have a go before the crowds get here!"

Georgie didn't remember being introduced to him, but she was accustomed to people in the RV world recognizing her knowing who she was from years of TV ads for the Johnny B. Goode RV Empire. She smiled back pleasantly. "Not right now —maybe later!"

He mimed disappointment, and she moved on.

She found Zachary in the first place she tried, prowling around the Big Top, keeping an eye on Ginger and the kids while he checked ropes, cables, machinery. Doyle was there too, helping Ginger put the kids through their paces, and on the other side of the ring, various performers tumbled, flew, and leaped their way through routines. She could see Angelique and Travis, working with a giant ball and a chair, balancing and flipping.

In the center, Cassandra was up high, twirling on a ribbon of silk. Rollo, sitting on an upturned box, was watching her.

He would be an anxious man. After one daughter had been badly injured, another was now performing the same sky-high feats.

Georgie waved to Ginger and Doyle and spent a few minutes perched on a seat, watching rehearsals. She didn't want to look too much as though she was seeking out Zachary. Right now, he was her secret weapon.

Trixxi sat quietly, her bright eyes taking in all the action. She turned her head and uttered a soft whine when Zachary worked his way around to them.

"Good girl." Zachary's massive paw smoothed over her head. "Well-behaved pooch." He took a seat beside Georgie and waved a hand at the action. "Are you here to watch the talent or find a saboteur?"

Georgie turned to look at him thoughtfully. "You think whoever it is might be here?" Her gaze swept around the ring. There were maybe a dozen performers going through their paces and five or six of the ground crew, including Zachary and Doyle. Plus Rollo.

"I wish I knew." He said nothing for a moment while his eyes moved from one person to the next. She noted that his gaze held for a moment when it reached Hugo, doing something to the thick supporting cables for the high wire.

He looked tense, she thought. "You still haven't seen anything in your crystal ball?"

"Oh, I have," he said, his voice rumbling even though he spoke in an undertone. She could hear the frustration. "Riddles."

Georgie had to laugh at that. "So I'm not the only one."

"Goes with the territory," he said. "For me, it's like peeling an onion. I see the first layer of meaning, then another, then deeper, still another. Everything dark, hidden in clouds, and then sudden illumination."

Intriguing, Georgie thought. *Dark and hidden?* That reminded her of how he had first appeared to her when he came to her gypsy trailer. Dark, mysterious depths. He had a different way of seeing. His crystal ball seemed to perform uniquely, too.

"I wonder if it's tied up with our personalities?" she said, staring at Cassandra, who was spinning so fast she was just a blur. "I see a mist, sometimes images. At other times I hear voices."

"And sometimes, you just *know*."

She half-turned, studying him. "How do you know that?"

"I can feel it." His dark eyes, fathomless, looked into hers, enough to make her swallow hard. She didn't know who or what Zachary was, but he could transmit more power in one glance than she could with hours of concentration.

He was right, though. Sometimes she did just

'know', and this time she was confident that Zachary was her best hope.

"OK." She waited for a beat and said, "So what did you see? Tell me about this riddle?"

"It could be best summed up," he said, "as an image of a never-ending flight of steps, disappearing into infinity."

"Oh." She couldn't help but grin at him. "Not the most useful guide to finding a saboteur."

He shook his head, his mouth twitching and a brief gleam of wry humor lighting his eyes. "No."

"It's no wonder that so many people think we're frauds, is it?" Georgie sighed and stretched her legs out in front of her. "So hard, sometimes, to get anything concrete. Do you have any suspicions at all?"

"Some."

He had said that before, she remembered, but wanted to see what she could find out by herself first.

"I brought my crystal ball with me," she said, pointing at the bag at her feet. "Do you want to see it?"

"Yes."

Georgie lifted the bag and withdrew her crystal ball, handing it to him still wrapped in its velvet cloth. Zachary unwrapped it just enough to see it without risking anyone else being able to see what he had in his lap. He nodded in approval. "That's better. Moonlight and earth; works every time." He stared down at the shining crystal surface, and the cleft in his forehead grew deeper. After a few long minutes, he dipped into his pocket and pulled out his crystal ball. As Georgie had done when they first met, he held both of the crystal spheres on his lap, his eyes moving from one to the other.

Then he sucked in a breath, and his head snapped up. He looked furious.

Georgie's heart gave a thump, and she clutched his arm. "Zachary? What is it?"

CHAPTER 9
Win the Bunny

Outside, Tammy followed the same path as Georgie, walking past the booths. To blend in with the circus theme, she was wearing an outfit similar to the one worn by Margy in *State Fair*. Sure, the circus wasn't quite the same as a state fair, but the Callaway sideshow alley reminded her of it.

Jerry had shaken his head when she ordered it online the week before. "Tams, we're just there to fix up a few teething problems," he had said. "You've already got enough outfits to last you a year without wearing the same one twice."

She had smiled at him sweetly. "And your point is?"

After a brief pause, he laughed. "Right. Ignore me."

"I will," she assured him and bought it anyway.

Her vintage clothes were her indulgence. They made her happy.

Today, she felt good. Very Margy-at-the-state-fairish, tripping along in her dress with the pretty embroidered pink bodice and the breeze playing with her full skirt and making the broad ribbon at her waist flutter. She had, however, opted for sensible pink flats instead of the white high heels favored by Margy. Recent rain had made the grass underfoot spongy.

Her steps slowed when she spotted Hugo standing outside the Wild West Shootout, his arms folded so that his biceps bulged in his black Callaway Circus crew member t-shirt. A glance around showed her that there was nowhere to hide. No crowd to melt into, as there would have been if the gates were open.

He saw her coming and waved her over, his face lighting up. "Tammy! Just the girl I wanted to see!" He took in her outfit, and he whistled. "Hoo-ee! Lookin' good, girl. Kinda old-fashioned, but nice."

With a silent groan, she pasted a smile on her face and stopped at the booth, nodding at the man who ran it. Tessa's husband, she remembered. "Hi, Bob."

"Hello." All business, he ran a box cutter around the tape sealing a cardboard box, and opened it up. "Here, Hugo, make yourself useful and put some of these on the top shelf."

"Sure." Obligingly, Hugo plucked out several plush toys, the perennial favorite for men who managed to dazzle their girlfriends with their shooting gallery prowess. "I saw your friend go by earlier," he said to Tammy. "With the white mutt."

White mutt? Her smile became fixed, and she felt her teeth grate. "You mean Georgie? With Trixxi? Great, that's who I was looking for. I'll see you later."

"What's the hurry?" Hugo held up a giant white bunny with a huge pink ribbon around its neck. "Have a shot at this first. See if you can win the bunny." He winked at Bob. "And if you can't, then I'll win it for you." He moved around behind the counter and tucked the bunny and a floppy doll into a vacant space on the top shelf. "There. Keep your eye on the prize."

Tammy was tempted to bat her eyelashes and simper. *Ooooh, you'll win the big bunny for l'il ole me?* Instead, she put her hands on her hips and grinned harder. "You win every time, do you?"

"Most times. When I'm not distracted." He came back out front, picked up one of the rifles, and held it out to her. "Go on, try it."

Tammy looked at the gun. It was tethered to the

stand in front of the targets: one of the modern fairground models, using a light beam to hit the targets instead of old-fashioned BB pellets. Still, a gun was a gun. She had shot skeet, paintballs, and targets; used rifles and handguns.

This wasn't a fair contest.

"You one of those women that don't like guns?" asked Hugo. "Don't worry; this isn't real. It uses light. Safer." He nodded at her, pushing it closer. "Go on."

Bob had paused in his unpacking to watch. His face told her that he wished Hugo would take a hike, but he was interested in what she might do anyway.

Tammy knew what they were both seeing: a girly girl dressed up in an outfit out of a past era, playing make-believe.

Not someone to be taken seriously.

There was nothing Tammy liked better than to turn people's expectations around.

"Gosh," she said, reaching out with a fingertip to touch the gun. "I don't know…what do I have to do?" She gazed helplessly at the gun and the shooting gallery.

"Just a sec." Hugo ducked back into the booth and flicked a few switches. "There. Aim for the ones on the bottom row. You'll probably miss at first until you get your eye in."

The moving belts with rows of targets started rumbling along on the bottom row: a row of tombstones with targets in the middle. Above them were smaller targets, moving slightly faster: silver stars on a black background. The back row had a western saloon theme: it featured playing cards and bottles that popped up in random spots at random times. LED lights flashed to show where to shoot.

Huh. Piece of cake.

"Look," Hugo said. "Let me show you."

He put the rifle to his eye, took a moment to aim, and then picked off three of the slow-moving tombstones in a row. "See? Easy." His chest visibly puffed out. "Gets harder when you get to the top row. Not many can do that."

"But you can?"

"Most times," he said nonchalantly. "You need eight or better out of ten to win the top shelf. The bunny's in the bag." He winked. "Your turn."

Out of the corner of her eye, Tammy saw Jerry wandering in her direction.

"Well…I guess I could have a go." She smiled at Bob and took the gun. "The bottom row first, you say?"

"Just take it slow," Hugo said. "Don't worry if you miss. Most first-timers do."

Tammy put the gun to her shoulder and squinted down the barrel. Then she switched to the other eye. She sighed and went back to the first eye.

"Don't overthink it," advised Hugo. "Just shoot."

Behind her, Jerry's voice said, "What are you doing, Tams? You know you hate guns."

She jumped convincingly, lowered the gun, and turned to him, biting her lip. "Hugo thought I should try."

"C'mon, man," Hugo said, frowning at the intruder. "Let the girl have some fun."

Jerry shrugged. "Not my problem if she wants to make a fool of herself."

"You think you could do better?"

"Nope," Jerry said genially. "Compared to Tams, I'm an amateur." Knowing that Hugo wouldn't understand the irony until Tammy had finished with him, he grinned. "Fire away, woman."

Tammy lifted the gun again and sighted it, aiming a little to the left of the moving tombstone. She fired and missed. Fired again and missed.

In the background, she could see Hugo smirking.

Six carefully engineered misses later, she had hit one tombstone, had her eye in, and was confident she could hit the random pop-ups on the top row.

"Wow!" she said, handing the gun to Hugo. "That was exciting!" She ran a hand underneath her waved hair and flipped it out while smiling at him prettily. Back to being a girly girl who couldn't shoot for nuts. "Can you show me how you hit the ones on the top now?"

Bob cleared his throat. "Fast or super-fast?" he asked Hugo.

"Just fast. I want to win that bunny for Tammy here. *Then* you can try super-fast." Hugo rolled his shoulders, planted his feet wide, and nodded. "Let's go."

The targets on the top row moved along faster. Hugo fired quickly, guessing at the placement of the targets, swinging the gun to pick them off. His score mounted on a bright panel right underneath the white bunny. One, two, three…in the end, seven.

"Durn it!" He pretended good-humored frustration, but Tammy could see annoyance in his eyes. "That was a warm-up round. I'll win it for you on the next."

"Thanks, but I need to go see Georgie." Tammy gave a regretful glance at her watch. "Could I have just one go at it myself before I do?"

Hugo and Bob exchanged a look, and then Hugo shrugged. "Sure, why not? Bob, slowest speed."

"No, no! Put it on the *fastest!*" Tammy said, giggling. "I'm gonna be, like, Annie Oakley!"

Jerry's mouth twitched, and he stood back to give her room.

Hugo shook his head, nodded at Bob, and leaned on the side of the booth to watch. "You go, girl!"

Tammy raised the rifle. *Just like skeet, only better,* she thought. She balanced lightly on her feet and waited. The bell sounded, and the targets started popping up.

She fired. The hit registered, and the bell rang again.

"Hot damn! Talk about beginner's luck!" Hugo slapped his knee.

Tammy kept firing, adjusting her pose and the gun sights the second the target registered in her field of vision. One, two, three... seven, eight, nine. She missed the tenth by a hair.

She lowered the gun and said to Jerry in a breathy voice, "Oh, that was so fun!" Putting the gun back on the front stand, she smiled at Bob. "Keep the bunny, Bob. It's gorgeous, but I have this white mutt that I'm kinda fond of."

Jerry put his arm around her shoulder. "See?" he said to Hugo. "I have no chance against this one. For a gal who hates guns, she's a mean shot."

Tammy beamed at Hugo. "Thanks. Let's have another competition soon!"

"Sure," he muttered and bent down to yank more prizes out of the box to load the shelf. "Any time." He glanced up at her, spite in his eyes. "You could have told me you knew how to shoot."

"You just assumed," Tammy said sweetly. "People tend to do that with me. So I mess with them a bit." She took Jerry's hand. "Let's go find Georgie."

They walked off, and when they were at a safe distance, Jerry remarked: "Always a pleasure to watch you in action, Tams."

She glanced up at him and felt a rush of affection. Jerry, her conniving, clever, con-man partner. He could annoy the heck out of her, but he was the one for her. Not that she planned on letting him feel too secure about that any time soon.

It paid to keep men like Jerry on the hop. `

"Together," she said, "we could make the perfect team. Run a long con. Wouldn't it be fun?" Then she added, "only those who deserve it, of course."

"Of course." He swung her hand companionably. "You've made an enemy there, Tams. Did you see his eyes?"

"Yes." She shrugged. "I didn't like him anyway. And we'll be gone in a few days. At least now he'll leave me alone."

"You'd better hope that he's not the saboteur," he said, a note of seriousness in his voice.

"You'll protect me." She batted her eyelashes. "My hero."

Jerry laughed. "Ah, Tams. I—"

He didn't get a chance to finish. There was a sound of rending metal and a series of crashes from inside the Big Top, followed immediately by panicked shouts.

They bolted for the entrance.

CHAPTER 10

Sabotage

When Zachary looked up from the crystal ball, Georgie thought that she had rarely seen such incandescent fury in another person's eyes. Zachary was a giant of a man, and his anger made him even more formidable. In her lap, Trixxi whined and trembled, her feet scrabbling.

Quickly, Georgie removed her hand from Zachary's arm and used it to stroke Trixxi soothingly. Her eyes went to the two crystal balls cradled in his big hands.

In hers, the mist was swirling rapidly, yet the surface was bright enough to hurt her eyes. She had never seen it like that. Zachary's smaller crystal ball was, in contrast, dark. It reminded her of Zachary himself, with a rich depth to the darkness that hinted of many layers.

Like peeling the layers off an onion, he had told her.

He regained control, and the passionate anger in his eyes faded, leaving his gaze cold when he met her eyes.

"Steps to infinity." He spared a moment to pat Trixxi apologetically and then gestured around him. "Look around. What do you see?"

She picked up his meaning immediately, flicking a glance around the Big Top with its tiered seating. VIP sections had comfortable theatre-style seating for special guests, and there were simple aluminum benches with vinyl cushions for cheaper seats. Steps and more steps…

Her heart thumping, she nodded. "Tell me."

"Steps. People falling, screams…steps collapsing." He hesitated. "The steps to infinity: I think that means we might have at least one death."

Georgie thought about some footage she'd seen on TV once, showing a stand collapsing at a football final. People had died then.

A small child could be crushed, killed.

This saboteur was cold and calculating. With injuries to spectators, the Callaway circus would face lawsuits, investigations, negative publicity. This was no longer just about the people who worked here.

Georgie looked at her watch. "A couple of

hours until showtime. Do you know which section?"

Zachary gave a grating laugh. "I don't even know if it'll happen today or next week. You know how it works."

She did, yet…impulsively, Georgie set Trixxi down at her feet and then reached across to pick up her crystal ball. "May I have yours too?"

Without comment, he passed it over.

Georgie placed both in her lap and put one hand on each, with trembling fingertips on the crystal surfaces. She closed her eyes.

It was like nothing she had ever felt before. She sucked in a deep breath as she sensed what Zachary had seen so clearly: the collapse of scaffolding, bodies tumbling to the ground.

Then, with a crashing sense of urgency, she got more.

Soon. It would be soon.

"It's today," she said, without opening her eyes, feeling her pulse racing. "It's…a man. I'm sensing a man." She couldn't get any images, just a vague outline of a male figure, gray and hazy. Someone skulking, looking around, with a deadly focus.

She concentrated but got nothing more. Frustrated, she frowned and tried letting go, letting her consciousness drift.

Nothing.

Georgie shook her head. "It's today, and we're looking for a man. He's determined, whoever it is. We're not going to stop him." Without consciously thinking about it, more words spilled from her. "He's devious. Good at hiding in plain sight."

At that, her eyes flew open. "I don't know what that means."

"Seemed pretty plain to me, but it's nothing I didn't suspect for myself. I've been watching for weeks, and if it were anyone obvious, I would have noticed by now."

The sounds of children laughing drew their attention to a curtained doorway about a third of the way around the tent. Ginger's daughter, Lucy, raced through it, her red braids flying, clutching something in her hands. Nicolas and Sam chased her while her small cousin Nora came in after them, yelling, 'Wait! Wait for me!"

Shrieking with laughter, Lucy scrambled up the seats, ran along, and swung down the other side like a monkey.

"Gonna get you!" Sam shouted, running underneath to cut her off. "Get her, Nic!"

Georgie hurtled to her feet. "No! *NO!*"

Zachary was already off and running, moving

amazingly quickly for such a big man. He, too, knew.

They were too late.

With a crash, the scaffolding collapsed on top of Sam and sent Nic flying off into the air, his tiny arms windmilling.

"I can't believe they're all OK. I can't believe it." Still pale, her eyes occasionally brimming with tears, Ginger sat huddled in the corner of her parents' RV, picking at a loose thread on the cuff of her sweater. "If I'd lost Lucy…"

Her mother gave her a quick hug and ruffled her hair. "You didn't. She's tough, like you." She had tempered her usually loud voice to soothe Ginger, but she was steaming.

They all were. Angry and afraid.

"I'm giving Zachary a raise." Attempting a smile, Theodora picked up her coffee and took a long draught. "He had the strength of ten men pulling that scaffolding off Sam. And to get everything back up again in time for the matinee…"

Georgie and Scott exchanged somber glances. No matter how quickly Zachary had moved, how strong he was, if the scaffolding hadn't collapsed in such a way as to form a protective barrier over Sam's head, the outcome could have been very different.

Rollo, looking more defeated than Georgie had seen him yet, spoke in a flat voice. "We're going to have to call in the police."

"No," Theodora said immediately. "It'll be the end of us."

Rollo shot her a look. "It could be the end of us if we *don't*. We can't risk lives."

"Not yet." Theodora didn't raise her voice, but she might as well have. The bottled-up anger and resentment made her deep voice vibrate. "Before the police, let's try something else. Let's call a meeting and tell everyone what's going on. Tell them all there's a traitor in our midst. Someone might have seen something; might suspect someone."

"And they'll all be paranoid, spying on each other," Rollo countered. "Morale will be zero."

"Some of them know what's going on now anyway," Ginger pointed out. "We weren't exactly being careful about what we were saying when the seats collapsed."

That was true, Georgie thought. Rollo had been beside himself with fear and rage, yelling about killing the bastard who had done this, while

Zachary, Doyle, and Jerry were heaving scaffolding aside and getting the kids out. Ginger was screaming; the kids were howling. Nobody believed it was an accident.

Scott spoke up. He and Jerry seemed to be thinking more clearly than any of the Callaways; they were all too shaken to reason things through. "Whoever is responsible did it last night, after the show."

Rollo nodded tiredly. "It happened even though we kept watch last night. Travis, Doyle, and my two boys. None of them saw anything."

Travis, Georgie thought immediately. She wanted to ask Rollo if he could entirely trust his nephew after the family split but bit her tongue. She'd find a better time to ask that.

Rollo groaned and rubbed his balding head. "What's a man to do? I don't know. Keep the police out of it, and someone could get killed. I'd never forgive myself. Bring them in, and the media will find out. They'll make it sound so bad that people will stay away in droves."

"What about Hugo? I've never liked that man," Ginger said. "He's creepy. Thinks he's God's gift to women."

"That's not a crime in itself," her father said.

"But we've been thinking about getting rid of him anyway; he's allergic to work."

Jerry looked at the list in his hand, people hired on by the Callaways in the past twelve months, and said what had been in Georgie's mind. "You've got eleven names here, including three new performers. You don't include Travis and Angelique. You're confident that they aren't involved?"

Rollo frowned. "I've known their father a long time. We were good friends, once."

"Ex-partners have been known to turn on each other," Jerry pointed out, his voice unemotional. "So have friends and family. Georgie's last case proved just that."

Georgie squirmed uncomfortably. "Don't call it a 'case'. I'm just a fortune-teller."

Theodora jumped in. "You do solve cases, though; I've read about it."

"That was accidental." There was no way Georgie was going to tell her about the Crystal Ball Investigation Team. They'd had some success, yes, but the name was tongue-in-cheek. "I'm not a private detective."

"You knew about the faulty seating," Theodora persisted. "I heard you say, to Jerry."

Georgie opened her mouth to give the credit to Zachary and then shut it again. Until they found who was responsible, he wanted to stay under the radar.

A soft knock came at the door, and Tessa's voice called from outside. "Teddy? Can I see you for a moment?"

They all exchanged glances. *Please,* thought Georgie. *Don't let anyone else have been hurt.*

Tessa was carrying several costumes draped over her arm. Georgie recognized them: the glittering silver outfits that Gaye and Marco had worn for their act.

"I'm sorry," Tessa said, her kind face creased in concern. "I know that this is the last thing you need right now. But these outfits… look at them." She came in and laid them on the table, stretching the fabric with both hands. "See how the seams have been weakened? Once Gay and Marco got into their act, they'd split. There are three other outfits, same treatment."

For a moment, nobody said anything. It all just seemed too much.

Georgie spoke up. "Who has access to wardrobe?"

"Pretty much anyone," Tessa said bleakly. "They're all kept in the dressing room, in boxes, and on hangers. People are in and out all the time: fire-walkers, clowns, tumblers." Although it was

Tessa's job to look after the performer's clothes, she didn't stay in the room continuously.

"All right." Theodora sagged, looking almost as defeated as Rollo. "Thanks, Tessa. You can fix them for tonight's show?"

"Easily," Tessa said. "But there's more. I'm sorry."

They all just looked at her.

"The chair for the high wire act. One of the legs has been loosened."

CHAPTER 11

Plans A, B and C

Just as Georgie and Scott sat down in Jerry's motorhome for a team discussion, a video call came in from Layla. She was wearing a red 50s bandana, with hair styled in Victory bangs. "I miss you guys," she said, sounding nostalgic. "I need my fix of the retro crowd. My little vintage trailer looks lonely all by itself next to Jaxx's monster RV." Her voice changed, becoming more heated. "And Jaxx Saxby is the presenter from *hell*. She's driving the team crazy."

Georgie grinned at the phone. "You didn't expect her to change, did you? We're all missing the retro scene ourselves. Not much of it here at the circus. But you know Tams; she found a State Fair outfit to wear and then out-performed a would-be Romeo at the shooting gallery yesterday."

Layla sighed rapturously. "She told me. What I wouldn't have given to see that."

Georgie turned the phone around to show Tammy, who currently wore 50s navy pedal pushers and a sailor top. "Say hello."

Layla waved. "Now that's what I'm talking about. My retro pal."

"How's Seth?" Georgie raised an eyebrow. "Is it worth putting up with Jaxx to catch up with him?"

"Almost." Then Layla smiled. "Well, yeah. But I don't know how this long-distance thing is going to survive. Working for a self-obsessed slave driver like Jaxx, he doesn't have time to visit me when I'm on the road. Anyway, I phoned to hear what's happening with your saboteur. I wish I could be there to help."

"We're having a meeting now," Georgie told her. "If we give you a list of names, can you do some digging to see what you can find out?"

"Absolutely. I'm bored. Seth's tied up all night processing video because Jaxx made them re-do this shoot with—no, you don't want to hear about that. So yeah, send it to me!"

"OK. Just plug the names into Google with keywords like 'circus' and 'Callaway' and see what you find."

"Yay." Layla punched the air and finished the call.

"Great, that will save us some time," Georgie said. She got the list from Jerry and sent it through.

Tammy made coffee for them all. "Since we're not going to get much sleep tonight, we might as well fill up on caffeine."

Jerry watched her, drumming his fingers on the table. "Are you sure you want to be in on this, Tams? Scott and I can stake them out between us."

Tammy gave him one of her scathing looks along with his cup of coffee. "I won't even bother to answer that."

"Whoever it is, is dangerous. And devious."

"And I'm not?"

Jerry gave up. It was hard to argue with a girl who had, not so long ago, raced to free him from the clutches of some prepper extremists. He went back to the list provided by Rollo. "We have eleven people who have joined the circus in the past twelve months. I've added a few more: Solly Starr's children, Travis and Angelique. Rollo doesn't believe that they – or Solly – would have a hand in this, but I'm not so sure."

"He gave Solly a quarter of a million dollars from his win, just for old times' sake," Georgie pointed out. "What motive would Solly have to send his children to sabotage the Callaway Circus? It's like killing the golden goose."

"Unless they sent someone else to do it," Scott said thoughtfully. "It seems the Starr children voluntarily came here to work rather than continue with the All Starrs. That meant they lost two of their best performers. Their own children defected to a circus that's always succeeded where they failed. That's got to hurt."

"Notice that Angelique and Travis haven't yet suffered in any way," Georgie added. "That's suspicious in itself." She glanced from Scott to Jerry. "You two have been doing all the planning on this. What's happening tonight?"

"One of us—including Tammy—shadows whoever is on Rollo's watch list, taking it in turns. One just patrols the grounds, being alert for anything and everything. The other will be resting; we'll take two-hour breaks."

Georgie nodded. She had been tempted to join them but had decided instead to stay in her trailer with her crystal ball, alert for any rise in temperature or changes in the light that indicated a message might be coming through.

She wasn't worried about dozing off: somehow, she knew that she'd sense it on a subconscious level if there was something she needed to know.

"What about Zachary?" asked Tammy, curling up her feet beneath her.

"It's a bit hard for him to hide, being the size he is, so he's volunteered to do a few extra patrols working in with the usual security guard," Georgie said. "Everyone is relieved; they're all a bit nervous after the stand collapsed. Plus, he's going to monitor his crystal ball too."

Jerry shook his head. "I still can't process a guy who looks like a Berserker staring into a crystal ball the size of an orange. Or carrying it around in his pocket. He looks like he should be yelling war cries and brandishing an ax."

"You haven't seen him when he's doing a reading." Georgie felt goosebumps at the memory of Zachary's intense stare; the depths upon depths in his eyes. "And by the way, have you seen him look at Ginger? I think he's smitten."

"Really?" Tammy perked up. "Big giant dark Zachary and tiny little Ginger. Interesting pair."

"Young Lucy loves him," Scott observed. "She makes a beeline for him whenever she sees him."

"So that's us, now for Rollo's night watch list." Jerry turned the sheet of paper over and ran his eye over the names. "He has Darcy on first watch tonight, right after the show finishes. He's relieved by Doyle at eleven, who will then swap with Oscar at one, followed by Travis at three and then Rollo at five, which is when people start waking up anyway."

"That's Plan A," Scott said. "Plan B kicks in tomorrow if we haven't nabbed anybody overnight —which we don't expect to happen, it must be said. It seems a bit soon for him to move again after rigging the seating to collapse."

"Not to mention the costumes and the chair," Tammy added. "Tessa's going to make sure the props and costumes are never left unattended now." She turned her attention to Georgie. "You're the Plan B girl, I understand."

"Plan B is simple. We go back to the reason I'm here: teaching Ginger how to read fortunes. Everybody knows about that. The idea is to call in different people so she can practice, but they'll all be from the list of people employed in the last twelve months—plus Travis and Angelique." She shrugged. "Who knows whether I'll pick up on anything. But Zachary will be in there too."

"Zachary?" Tammy laughed. "In your gypsy trailer, along with you and Ginger and whoever's having a reading? You'll need a shoehorn."

"No, we're doing it in Ginger's new gypsy trailer, not mine. Hers is a bit bigger, with an extra bench seat."

Jerry frowned. "Won't people be wondering why Zachary's there?"

"Not when they see him fixing the cupboards and adding a new shelf," Georgie said smugly. "He'll fade into the background. Just the handyman; they're used to seeing him around doing odd jobs."

Jerry took a swig of his coffee. "And if Plans A and B both fail to get a result, Rollo has Plan C."

Georgie guessed it before he went any further. "Call in the police?"

He nodded. "Call in the police."

They all hoped that wouldn't be necessary.

CHAPTER 12

The Fake Fortune-Teller

That night, everyone Rollo assigned to night watch did their patrols without incident, checking the grounds at random times, following different routes. The CBI team shadowing them was alert for anyone who put in only a token effort, as you might expect from a saboteur who knew nothing was going to happen, but nobody behaved suspiciously.

Georgie texted Ginger and Zachary at breakfast: *Plan B good to go. Nine o'clock OK?*

Both sent back a *yes*, and by nine-fifteen, Zachary was busy with his tools at the back of the gypsy trailer, while Ginger sat nervously by Georgie's side, staring at the crystal ball.

"I don't have to try doing a reading in front of people, do I?" she asked.

"No, don't worry," Georgie assured her. "I'll run it like a teaching session. I'll explain to you how I do a reading, what I'm looking for, how to put people at ease, and so on."

Ginger cast a glance at Zachary, perched on a stool in front of an upended drawer, tools at the ready. "I'm glad you're here, Zach. I know nobody is likely to attack me here, but anybody who'd set up an accident like mine...I can't help being scared."

"Happy to be of service," Zachary said, his voice sounding even more gravelly than usual as he nodded at her.

Georgie's eyes met Zachary's, and she smiled. As yet, nobody in the Callaway Circus knew about the small, unique crystal ball he kept in the pocket of his cargo pants. To them, he was just a good, reliable worker and a formidable bodyguard.

While waiting for Robbie Keefe, one of the road team, Georgie scrolled through the text messages from Layla one more time. They had a busy day lined up: all thirteen people on the suspects list had agreed to help Ginger practice her fortune-telling skills. Georgie had included the two that had come from All Starr's Circus—especially after Layla had unearthed a nugget of information about Angelique that had been buried deep in social media. Angelique, it seemed, had a reputation for petty and sometimes vicious acts of retalia-tion to those who crossed her. Layla had been awake half the night, digging into Facebook pages and Twitter accounts, following links, and friending people she barely knew.

It took over an hour for Georgie to sift through the information Layla had sent through about the Callaway Circus members, following the trail to various web pages and old newspaper files. She paid out a fair whack in subscriptions to get to old arti-cles on file, but it was worth it to get a clear picture of the people who would be coming through her door for a reading.

Angelique Starr, she mused. A talented performer who could easily dress in dark clothes and glide through the night undetected. But would she know how to sabotage a water pump? Would she have the strength to loosen wheel nuts? With a torque wrench, yes. Unless she was working with someone else. Like Travis.

Hugo Metcalfe, the circus Romeo, had a spotty work history and had been involved in petty crime. He had come to the Callaways via word of mouth from other traveling shows and had worked briefly for All Starrs fifteen months before. Could the Starr family have hired him to sabotage the show?

Robbie Keefe, their first customer, was a buddy

of Hugo's and was another one with a murky past. There was nothing in his record that would have stopped Rollo from hiring him, though, and he was a good enough road hand. Still, for enough money, someone like Robbie could be enticed to play on the wrong side of the law.

In the early hours of the morning, the last batch of notes through from Layla had finished with: *"still digging…stay posted."*

Footsteps sounded outside, and Robbie knocked on the doorframe and poked his head inside. "Hello?"

"Come in, Robbie." With a smile intended to put him at ease, Georgie pointed to the folding chair on the other side of the table. She and Ginger were sitting together on the bench seat. "Thanks for coming. You're Ginger's first customer!"

He settled into the chair, deliberately sprawling out. "So, what does the future hold for me? Do your worst!"

Ginger's pale face flushed with embarrassment. "I'm not doing much today. Georgie's teaching me."

The look in his eyes changed to one of speculation. "What do I have to do?"

"You can ask questions if you want, but you don't have to. You can just wait and see what comes up." Georgie moved into teaching mode. "Ginger, sometimes people who come to see you will be passive. They'll just want you to tell them things. Sometimes they'll be aggressive, challenging you to prove yourself."

"Oh, God." Ginger looked sick. "I can't do this."

"Yes, you can." Georgie slid easily into her planned approach: explaining to Ginger how to ad-lib if she didn't know anything. "I'll show you how to draw information out of people." She winked at Robbie. "This is all classified under trade secrets, Robbie. No telling people how we pull it off!"

The plan was that the first of Ginger's guinea pigs would go back and report to the others that Georgie B. Goode, Gypsy Fortune-Teller, was more into fakery than genuine readings. That, she figured, should put the saboteur at his or her ease.

Robbie just raised an eyebrow, waiting. His eyes rested briefly on the crystal ball, which just sat there reflecting the colors around it.

"See the look on Robbie's face?" Georgie asked Ginger. "He's determined not to give away anything. So you start with generalities." She drew the crystal ball closer. "You can spend a few seconds staring into the crystal ball and say things like, "You've worked hard all your life. Nothing has come easily; you've had to fight for everything you have."

"That's for sure," Robbie agreed.

"See?" Georgie said. "You can make that assumption because Robbie's one of the road crew, and he *does* work hard. Also, most people think they work too hard."

"I don't just think I do," he said. "I *know* it."

"Now you've got him involved," Georgie pointed out. "He agrees with you. So your next step would be to say something like, "Your present job is just a step on the path. Within six months, you'll be moving on to a stage in your life where you're getting what you truly deserve.""

Despite himself, Robbie looked interested. "Is that for real, or are you making it up?"

Georgie had to bite her lip to stop herself from laughing. In the crystal ball, she could see a mist forming, wispy, barely there. She knew that Robbie Keefe would indeed get what he deserved, but it was unlikely to be riches. She could sense his life stretching into the future, with Robbie always looking for the easy road to riches, never quite finding it.

The story of so many people's lives.

She answered his question. "This time, I'm making it up, but it's true of many people."

He peered more closely at the crystal ball. "It's changing. Going kind of frosty. How does it do that?"

"It's just a property of the crystal it's made of," she lied. "The trailer warms up quickly with four people in it. It's reacting to changes in temperature, but it looks effective, doesn't it?"

"Huh. That's what I thought," he said, leaning back. "It's just a racket."

Good, Georgie thought. That was precisely what she wanted him to report back.

When the saboteur walked through her door, she wanted him—or her, although she felt it was a male—to be confident that there was nothing to fear here.

The morning wore on, with a new candidate every fifteen or twenty minutes. When one person finished, they went to find the next.

By lunchtime, they had been through eight on the list, starting with Robbie and finishing with Angelique.

"You know," Ginger said, watching Angelique's back as she walked away, "she might be talented, but I can't warm to her. I wish Dad hadn't taken her on."

Georgie sat back and stretched. "Your father feels guilty, I expect. He's got a thriving business, a good reputation, and now he's set for life with the lottery win. What would you have done in his place if the children of your ex-business partner, your old friend, came and asked for a job?"

"They *had* a job. With their mother and father. If it were me, I would have stuck with my parents and tried to help them make it work." Ginger glanced at Georgie. "Dad did give them money, you know. To help them breathe new life into the All-Starrs."

"I know, he told me. A quarter of a million dollars is very generous since he owed Solly nothing."

Ginger shrugged. "He's always felt guilty about the All Starr Circus having such bad luck. Two hundred and fifty grand wasn't much out of twenty-seven million, he said, but it might help to pay for a few good performers. He's given away more than that, too."

"And did it make a difference?"

Ginger smiled wryly. "You'd think it would, but their reaction was odd. As though we were handing out charity, and they resented it, even though they took it. And then when Angelique and Travis came here, Solly blamed Dad."

"I can see why." Georgie sighed. "Your father was between a rock and a hard place. Imagine his predicament: does he give Angelique and Travis work and help their career, or does he say no, so the Starr circus keeps their star performers?"

"And the worst of it is, nobody's happy. Angelique and Travis are fighting with their parents, their parents are mad at Dad, and the troupe here at Callaway's have their noses out of joint because two new people are taking some of the spotlight." Ginger looked at her watch. "I'll have to go find Lucy, have some lunch. Doyle's had the kids all by himself this morning, with Tessa spotting."

Feeling hungry herself, Georgie stood up. "Lunch sounds like a good idea. We'll start again at two, with Hugo."

"And won't *that* be fun?" Rolling her eyes, Ginger stood. "I'll catch you later." She nodded at Zachary. "Thanks for being the bodyguard, Zach. Bit of a waste of time for you."

"Happy to be of service." He smiled at her, his eyes warm. "See you later." He stood up and went to the door, watching her walk briskly in the direction of her motorhome.

Georgie smiled to herself. "So, Zachary," she said casually. "When we find the saboteur and kick his butt from here to Hawaii, are you going to stick around and take your chances with Ginger?"

He turned and stared at her. Then his mouth quirked in an unwilling smile. "Too much to hope for that someone with the Sight wouldn't pick up on that."

"Exactly." Smugly, she beamed back at him. "And your answer is…?"

"Probably."

"Good. She needs someone like you."

He nodded. "She does."

"I think we did a good job of convincing everyone that I'm mostly fake, don't you?"

He laughed, warming to her. "Obviously, the word had spread by the time Angelique got here. Snooty little upstart."

Georgie grew more serious. "What are your feelings about the eight we've had in here so far?"

"It's none of them."

"Not Angelique?"

"No." He came over to the table and flipped open the cover of her notepad, where she'd written the names of everyone they were seeing. Eight were crossed out, with "NO" written beside them except for Angelique, who had a question mark. "You're not sure?"

"I don't think she could do it, but we haven't seen Travis yet, and she could be an unwitting accomplice."

He stood still for a moment, staring into the distance, then shook his head. "No, not her."

They both looked at the remaining five names.

Then Georgie's phone rang.

Layla had more news. Georgie put the phone on speaker, and as she talked, she and Zachary stared at each other.

"This," Georgie said, echoing both their thoughts as she hit the 'off button, "could change everything."

Zachary nodded. "Best not to tell Ginger."

"I was about to say the same thing. She won't be able to hide her feelings."

Georgie slid out of her seat. "I'll go tell Scott and grab some lunch. I don't know if I'll be able to eat, though. Who would have thought?"

CHAPTER 13

Revenge

Right on two o'clock, Hugo swaggered in. Instead of sitting on the chair like everyone else, he turned it around and straddled it, folding his arms over the backrest, so his biceps bulged. "Am I gonna be rich, with a tall, dark stranger in my future?" he asked Ginger. "Preferably one whose name is Miss January?" He laughed at his own wit.

Ginger eyed him with barely-concealed dislike. "Is that really what you want to know, Hugo?"

He settled more comfortably onto the chair and rested his chin on his forearms. "I'm open to anything. Try me."

She eyed him thoughtfully. "You feel you're not being paid what you're worth here; that your skills are not being utilized. You could probably be an actor, play roles in action movies. Like Bruce Willis, Tom Cruise."

Hugo looked startled and then pleased. "You're right; I could." Then a hint of suspicion entered his eyes. "Robbie told me that you say stuff like that, just to warm people up. Tell them they work hard and they're not appreciated." His gaze shifted to Georgie. "It's all part of the show."

"You're right: that's what I've told Ginger to say, if it takes a while for the real information to come flowing in," Georgie pacified him. "But in your case, it's true." She let her eyes rest on his biceps. "You take care of yourself, and you like talking to people. You'd probably make an excellent actor."

"You think so?" He sat up straighter.

"Oh, yes. Don't *you?*"

"I've been saying it for years." Hugo started to elaborate and barely drew breath for the next fifteen minutes. By the time he left to swap places with Doyle, he was convinced that nothing less than an Oscar lay in his future.

As his footsteps died away, Ginger put her head in her hands and groaned. "If I had even been *thinking* that I might do this, that would be enough to make me run a mile." She looked at Georgie. "Do you get many like him?"

"Enough," Georgie said ruefully. "Mostly, I just

tell them what they want to hear."

"Only four more to go. Thank goodness. After that, I'm never going to do this again."

Georgie laughed and got up to refill their water glasses. In the background, she saw Zachary quietly get his crystal ball out of his pocket and set it where he could see it, on a shelf over the drawers he was supposed to be fixing. He glanced at her and raised one eyebrow briefly.

Nerves had Georgie's heart beating faster.

This could be it.

Doyle Arrowsmith bounded up the step and into the trailer, smiling around easily. "Hey Ginger, Georgie. All set?" He nodded at Zachary, eyeing the drawers. "Problems?"

Zachary started screwing on a drawer runner that he'd had on and off a dozen times already that day. "Nothing I can't fix. Almost done."

Doyle looked at the seat in front of the table, turned it around the right way, and sat on it properly, his eyes glimmering with humor. "Hugo tells me that he's destined for the movies."

Ginger heaved a sigh. "The sooner Hollywood realizes his potential, the better. Then we can hire someone who will actually *work*." She beamed at Doyle. "I won't be able to tell you anything of value, of course. Georgie's mantra is "fake it till you make it".

Georgie broke in before Ginger started telling Doyle that the whole thing was a setup to unmask the saboteur. "Let's run through it, Ginger, so Doyle can see what you'd be doing if you *were* to take on the fortune-telling job."

"Which I'm not." She rolled her eyes at Doyle. "How were the kids this morning?"

"Great. Guess who nailed the backflip off the beam?"

"Not Nora?"

"Nora. That kid just won't give up. She's going to be one of the best."

"Yes!" They slapped hands in an enthusiastic high-five.

"Hey, you two," Georgie said, rapping on the table. "Save the chat for later. School is in session. Ginger, see if you can remember what to say."

In front of her, the crystal ball filled with mist.

"See that?" Ginger pointed to it and parroted Georgie's lies from earlier. "The crystal ball is reacting to temperature fluctuations, but it *looks* like there's something mysterious happening."

"Yeah?" He peered closer. "OK, off you go. Tell

me my fortune, then."

"I'll start, Ginger," Georgie said swiftly. "One technique you can use is to ask a customer actually to touch the crystal ball—just lay hands on it for a few moments—and hold a question in mind. That way, they're engaging with it." She smiled at Doyle. "Not every fortune-teller allows people to do that, but I occasionally do. Want to try it?"

"Sure."

He laid his hands on the crystal ball, his palms touching the curved surface.

Immediately, Georgie recoiled, feeling swamped by dark emotions and resentment. He had powerful shields, locked down tightly over his real feelings, so he presented an entirely different persona to the everyday world. If he hadn't laid hands on the crystal ball, she wouldn't have felt a thing.

Doyle was occupied staring at the crystal ball, not her, so she risked a glance at Zachary.

His eyes were fixed on his small crystal ball, which had turned jet black.

Her stomach flipped.

Striving to show nothing of her own emotions, she continued, her voice level.

"Keep repeating the question in your mind, Doyle, and then Ginger will see if she can pick anything up." She laughed lightly. "What she'll be doing is studying your face and trying to figure out what you want to know."

Doyle laughed too, grinned at Ginger, and then sobered, staring intently at the crystal ball. His face was unreadable.

She felt an odd pulse of power from Zachary's direction, and in response, the mist in her crystal ball turned gray. Then, sliding effortlessly into her mind, came an understanding of what Doyle wanted to know. She didn't hear it in Doyle's voice, and she didn't receive exact words—but she knew.

How long until my mother is avenged?

She swallowed. Layla had been right.

Ginger decided to join in, enjoying her lesson much more with Doyle rather than Hugo or Angelique. "Doyle, I sense that you're wondering about your future—whether it will work out for you, the work you're doing here as a clown, working with young performers. Or is there something else out there for you?"

Doyle flashed her a glance, and for a second, his eyes narrowed. Georgie realized that in a round-about way, Ginger *had* homed in on some of his thoughts - just not in the way she had intended.

Ginger's face, though, was full of innocent fun, and he relaxed. "Was that a lucky guess?" he asked. "Or am I that transparent?"

Ginger breathed on her nails and buffed them against her shoulder before saying in a sonorous voice, "I am Gypsy Ginger. You can hide nothing from me."

Thank goodness we didn't tell her, Georgie thought. There was no way Ginger would have been this convincing if she'd known what they suspected.

"Well done, Gypsy Ginger. Can I take my hands off the crystal ball now?"

Ginger waved her a hand carelessly. "If you like. I have now established a connection. You have no secrets from me."

"Don't overplay it, Ginger," Georgie advised. "Your clients might take it as a challenge."

"Oh, it's only Doyle." She put both hands to her forehead and closed her eyes. "I see you training a troupe of new clowns. All gifted athletes. A new act."

"The thought has entered my mind," Doyle said, smiling. "As you already know."

Georgie spoke again. "I can see this isn't going to work. You two know each other too well. Ginger, let me demonstrate another technique, where you encourage customers to talk about their past and use what they say to make logical guesses."

She drew the crystal ball back closer to her and

brushed her fingers across the surface. It still seemed to hold Doyle's imprint.

So much negative energy, she thought. Tonight, she'd be putting her crystal ball out in moonlight again to cleanse it.

"You were always an active child," she said. "An extrovert, I think?" That was a fair enough guess, considering Doyle had become a gymnast and a clown.

"Yes, that was me all right." There was a faint edge to his voice, although his smile remained easy; his eyes warm and friendly.

It was time to weave in some of the material Layla had unearthed.

Pretending to focus intently on the swirling mist in the crystal ball, she nodded. "Your parents…they weren't born into a circus environment, I feel."

"Good guess."

"But your father was a clown," Ginger broke in. "Didn't he do school shows or something while he was raising you?"

"You already know that." He shook a finger at her. "Doesn't count in a reading."

Georgie took a deep breath. "Your mother… something happened to her, I think. Many years ago. An accident of some kind?" She glanced up at him. "I sense she has passed away now."

"Yes and yes." His voice sounded cool.

"You became determined to do what she had never done," Georgie said, passing her hand theatrically over the crystal ball. "Achieve success, win an audience. She always felt you would be the one to carry the torch, so to speak."

Ginger interrupted again. "That's clever, Georgie. I can see what you're doing. Lots of parents want their children to succeed where they failed. And you said that she *felt* that Doyle would be the one to succeed, not that she actually *told* him. So he couldn't say it wasn't true, could he?"

"Wow," Doyle said, looking impressed. "So that's how you do it." He flashed a grin. "I might even take up fortune-telling myself, Ginger, if you don't want to do it."

He was a cool customer, Georgie acknowledged. There was no sign, on the surface, that he was anyone other than he pretended.

In the background, Zachary had silently risen to his feet and edged closer, out of Doyle's line of sight.

Time to close in.

Georgie turned to Ginger. "You can see how a fake would do it, can't you? But I did inherit some small talent from the gypsy side of my family, so let's see if I can pick up anything that would help

Doyle." She rubbed her hands together and smiled sweetly at Doyle. "One last effort."

She felt a roiling cloud of antagonism, but Doyle simply gave an easy shrug. "Sure. Then I'd better get back. There's a routine I need to go through with the other clowns before the show tonight."

"I'll be quick." Georgie touched the crystal ball lightly again and said, "Your mother. I don't know why, but I have the feeling that she *did* run away to join the circus." She cast a puzzled look at Doyle. "Does that sound right?"

"I think there was a circus in her past, way back," he agreed. "She never said a great deal about it."

Into Georgie's mind flashed a vivid image of an older, ravaged woman, bottle in hand, drunkenly berating a teenage boy.

Doyle's mother had never *stopped* talking about it. The injustice, as she saw it, ruined her life.

And, along with it, Doyle's.

"She was just a teenager," Georgie went on. "With strict parents. A circus came to town, and she traveled with it for a while. She had a natural aptitude for tumbling, balance, all the things you're good at."

Doyle, watching her closely, said nothing.

"She fell, I think. I feel that she suffered fairly serious injuries. When she recovered, she left the circus with one of the other performers." She glanced up at Doyle. "Your father."

"That's the story I grew up with," he agreed. "Hey, you're not bad. Unless you read about it somewhere, and you're just pretending you saw it in that thing." The last word was uttered with a short nod towards her crystal ball.

"It's a bit of both, Doyle," she admitted, her heart hammering. "A friend of mine found an old article about the fall that caused your mother's injuries." She paused. "At Callaway's Circus, thirty years ago."

Ginger's eyes widened. "*This* circus? Really?"

"You wouldn't have known," Georgie told her, watching Doyle. "Doyle used his grandmother's maiden name to get a job here." She paused for effect. "Just a month or so before *your* accident."

Ginger picked up on the tension in the air and became very still. She stared at Doyle. "Arrowsmith isn't your real name?"

"I didn't want your parents to feel that they owed me anything because of my mother," Doyle said. "I prefer to make my way in life."

"My friend also came across a Facebook post," Georgie went on. She was conscious that Zachary had moved to stand right behind Doyle, his face grim. The man moved as silently as a ghost. "On the page of someone called Crispian the Clown. It was posted the day your mother passed away."

Doyle's face was set like stone.

Looking him in the eye, Georgie said, "You vowed revenge."

"It was just after the wake. I was drunk." He shook his head. "Life goes on; I know that. And this show must go on too, so I'd better get moving." He pushed his chair back to go but came up against Zachary, standing like a mountain behind him.

"Doyle?" Ginger had gone very pale, her freckles standing out against her fair skin. "My accident. Please, it wasn't you…was it? Tell me it wasn't."

"Of course, it wasn't me!" He squirmed around and looked up at Zachary, his affable mask slipping. "What is this? Get out of my way!"

"*You.*" Zachary's eyes were bottomless, worlds of darkness within. "All the time, it was you." He clamped his hands on Doyle's arms and looked at Georgie, and in a low, threatening rumble, said just two words: "Plan C."

CHAPTER 14

Strawberries and Champagne

Four days later, Rollo hosted a farewell breakfast in the annex to his motorhome before the Johnny B. Goode RV Empire team hit the road.

"Strawberries and champagne. Nice," Georgie said to Theodora. "Pity we're all driving!"

"You are, we're not," she chirped. "But all of you are getting a bottle of the best to take with you." She pointed at five extravagant baskets wrapped in gold cellophane, adorned with glittering spirals of ribbon. "And one for your friend who found out about Doyle."

"Layla," Georgie said. "Thanks. She'll be thrilled."

Rollo was standing beside his wife, his face clear of worry for the first time in days. "You're all VIPs, any time you want to see the show. We can't thank you enough."

Theodora gave a hearty laugh. "We knew what we were doing when we picked Johnny B. Goode for our new RVs. Must be the only company in the country that includes a psychic detective with the guarantee!" She poked Georgie in the arm. "Sure I can't persuade you to travel with the circus?"

Georgie's eyes went straight to Zachary, standing on the other side of the room with Ginger. Feeling her gaze, he glanced across and raised his glass. The champagne flute looked far too delicate for his big hand. "You already have a fortune-teller," she pointed out. "Zachary's ten times better than I'll ever be."

She thought of the way their two crystal balls had worked together, the strange fusion of power. It kind of freaked her out.

Theodora's forehead creased momentarily as her gaze followed Georgie's. "Hmmm. Who would have thought." She had scoffed at the idea of Zachary, the quiet giant and Jack-Of-All-Trades, taking over the job intended for Ginger —until Georgie persuaded him to do a demonstration reading. "I still don't know how he did that."

"He has the Sight," Georgie said firmly. "It's not a trick."

"Zachary the Great. We'll need a bigger gypsy trailer. He can't fit in the one we had for Ginger."

"Easily done," Georgie said.

Theodora's eyes moved from Zachary to Ginger and back again, and a smile curved her lips. "We may need to trade Ginger's motorhome in on a bigger one, too."

"I think you may be right."

"She's talking about starting up a Callaway Circus summer school for kids. Tumbling, flying, contortionists." Theodora's shrewd eyes swung back to Georgie. "Says it was your idea."

"I got the idea from Doyle," Georgie admitted quietly. "He said his father worked in one."

"Doyle." Rollo's voice was filled with loathing. "I still can't get my head around what he did to our little girl. That accident of his mother's—it was caused by her own carelessness, and my Dad did everything he could for her."

Georgie nodded. "I know." She had already heard the whole story, but Rollo kept going over and over it. He had been in his early twenties at the time, and there had been a brief romance with Doyle's mother before Theodora had won his heart.

Over the years, Doyle's mother, a bitter and resentful woman, had twisted events in her own mind and poisoned her son against the Callaways. Turning to prescription drugs and alcohol, she had not had a peaceful death.

"The police may not have enough to charge him. Nobody saw anything, and he's not admitting it." Rollo sounded disgusted.

Jerry, Tammy, and Scott joined them in time to hear what he said.

"If there's anything to find, they'll dig it out," Jerry said. "Sometimes, it takes years." He clapped Rollo on the back. "Meanwhile, you can take your show on the road without worry. Just look at that." He gestured at the ranks of bright trailers and motorhomes, emblazoned with circus artwork and the big top rising behind them. "The Callaway Flying Circus and Carnival. All yours."

"With some of the best acts in the country," Tammy added.

Pride lit Rollo's face. "You're right. Yes, you're right. It's a top outfit; I've got four great kids and even more talent coming through with the grandkids. We're blessed."

Theodora gave him a resounding kiss on the cheek. "It's about as good as it gets, Rollo. As good as it gets."

A NOTE FROM THE AUTHOR

I hope you have enjoyed the circus setting in *As Good as it Gets*, the seventh book in the "Georgie" series, and seeing a very different fortune-teller at work in Zachary! I have to say I really enjoyed researching this one—what a great excuse to watch entertaining online videos of circus performances!

The next book in the series is *Good Golly Miss Molly*. (Now honestly, who could resist that as a title for a book?) So, who is Miss Molly? A lively 72-year-old who gets a huge kick out of the retro scene and everything associated with it—the clothes, the hairstyles, the dances and especially her newly-renovated vintage trailer!

Tammy, Georgie and Layla are thrilled with her reaction to their carefully-planned surprise, but their joy turns to concern when Rosa—an unexpected guest at the vintage trailer rally—tells them bluntly that sweet Miss Molly is in big trouble. Read the preview in this book!

Here's an invitation for you: subscribe to my newsletter to get news of new releases, bonus books, specials and a sneak peek at scenes from my books in progress. As a welcome gift, you'll also receive a copy of *Fortune's Wheel*, the prequel to the Georgie series.

Here's your chance to find out more about the intriguing old woman that Georgie sees as a kind of taciturn genie. Whether she wanted to believe it or not, from birth Georgie was destined to follow in Great-Grandma Rosa's footsteps—as well as inherit her crystal ball!

If you haven't already done so, visit my website below to join other readers and download your copy.

MargMcAlister.com/free-georgie-book/

ABOUT THE AUTHOR

Marg McAlister is the author of the popular Georgie B. Goode Cozy Mystery series (set in the USA) and Series 2 (Australian RV Adventure series), also featuring Georgie.

Marg lives by the sea on the mid-north coast of NSW, but she and her husband spend part of the year on The Gemfields in Central Queensland, living off the grid on their mining claim. While her husband digs for sapphires and zircons, operates the wash plant and drives around dirt tracks, Marg is usually writing—or socializing!

Marg is also the author of a series of books for aspiring writers, and the owner of Blue Gem Publishing, which publishes books in a range of genres.

Next in This Series
GOOD GOLLY MISS MOLLY

Chapter 1

"Here they come," said Georgie, clutching Tammy's arm and pointing. "Have you ever seen more of a contrast? Oh my goodness!"

"About time! I thought they'd never get here." Tammy grinned at the sight of Molly Kane, a short woman in her seventies with her white hair fixed in an age-defying ponytail and clad in a colorful 50s swing skirt, bustling along beside Georgie's tall, skinny great-grandma Rosa in her plain black blouse and skirt. "I'd love to have been a fly on the wall when those two met."

"At least Molly's happy. Not sure about Rosa," observed Layla, standing on the other side of Georgie. "And why does Jerry have that peculiar look on his face?"

"Probably because Miss Molly has talked his ear off all the way," Tammy guessed. "And maybe because she made him load up boxes of her favorite vintage clothes."

Jerry and his two charges were winding their way through the crowd to get to them. It wasn't speedy progress since Jerry was popular with the vintage trailer set. Ever since he had taken up with Tammy, almost a year ago now, his fan base had grown. Molly knew lots of those at the rally, too, and stopped to chat to every second person she encountered. Most of the rally people were from towns scattered throughout Missouri, so they saw each other fairly often.

Patiently stopping and starting to keep pace with Molly, Rosa didn't appear to be saying anything at all. Even from where she was standing, Georgie could see her keen dark eyes observing and assessing the whole scene: the people, the colorful vintage trailers against the backdrop of the north-east Missouri hills, and no doubt every table, chair, and mat arranged in conversation groupings. However, although Rosa wasn't smiling, she didn't have her prune face on, either.

Standing beside Georgie, Tammy was positively vibrating with excitement. She wasn't the only one; people at the rally who knew what was in store for Molly were quietly drawing near to watch her reaction. They had all seen the refurbished trailer, had exclaimed in delight and chatted while Georgie, Tammy, and Layla set up the cheerful outdoor living area in front of it. Expectant smiles showed on every face.

Jerry finally made it to the trailer, ushering Rosa and Molly before him. Georgie wasn't surprised to hear Rosa's name mentioned in a few low whispers, because she was rarely seen in public. A good many of them knew who she was, thanks mainly to Jaxx Saxby's new *Unsolved Mysteries* show. There was quite a buzz about who Jaxx's "secret psychic" might be. Some people were sure that it was Georgie. Others shook their heads and whispered knowingly: "No, no. It's Rosa—you know the old great-grandmother? The one who's been a gypsy, like, forever?"

Miss Molly spotted them and immediately rushed forward with her arms outstretched. "Tammy!" She flung herself at her target and hugged her close. Tammy laughed, lifting the diminutive septuagenarian off her feet. "Good *golly*, Miss Molly—I thought you'd never get here! I've been *dying* to see you again."

Miss Molly stood back and swung both of Tammy's arms out wide, taking her in with one admiring look; the short blonde Doris Day bob teamed with a cheerful sunshiny yellow dress with a row of tiny buttons. "I know that dress…that movie. *Caprice*, right? Don't you look great!" She nodded approvingly, her eyes resting on the dramatic sunglasses with black and white checked frames, and smiled, pinching Tammy's cheek. "Just look at that glow. That's what being in love will do for you." She aimed a backward glance at Jerry, her eyes twinkling. "So, you've taken up with this rogue, have you? I hope you're keeping him in line." She laughed, a rolling chuckle that instantly endeared her to everyone who met her. "I've been warning him what will happen if he doesn't treat you right."

Around them, everyone joined in the laughter. They all knew Jerry's reputation as a ladies' man, but he'd been with Tammy now for just over a year, and everyone now assumed he was off the market.

Molly dropped Tammy's hands and moved to Georgie, wrapping her in the same warm hug. "And you, too, Georgie—young Jerry here tells me that you're seeing a fellow from Australia? I hope that doesn't mean that we're going to lose you, taking off overseas somewhere." She stood back with a happy sigh, gazing around her, nodding and waving at faces she recognized. "Hi, Alice! Hi Dottie… Marjorie… everyone! I'll catch up with you all soon. It's so good to be here! I was getting sick to death of sitting around looking at myself, waiting for these old knees to heal." She bent down and gave each knee a quick pat and merrily executed a quick one-two jive step. "But now they're all tuned up and ready for action!" She turned around to

Jerry, who was carrying her compact suitcase. "Very well, Jerry, where's my trailer? I can't wait to see what the old girl looks like now." She twinkled at him. "I'll do a quick check to see if the repairs are up to scratch, stow this suitcase, and then it's nothing but fun!"

Georgie and Tammy exchanged a smile of pure delight. This was the moment they had been waiting for.

"It's all ready for you, Molly," Tammy said. "Come and take a quick look, and then it'll be time for you to sit down, have a coffee, and gossip." She and Georgie stepped apart, revealing the cute little outdoor setting in blues and pinks and reds. The door to Molly's brand new trailer stood open.

It was, for all intents and purposes, new. Jerry and the team back at the RV empire had stripped it and made sure every new cupboard—true to the original—opened and closed perfectly. The retro-look cooker was brand new too.

But it was the work that Georgie and Tammy and Layla had done that would undo Miss Molly, and they all knew it.

Tammy made a sweeping gesture with her hand. "Drum roll…! Here it is—all ready for you to move in."

Molly's face was a picture. If Georgie and

Tammy had orchestrated it themselves, they couldn't have asked for a better reaction. The color actually left her face for a moment, causing Tammy to step forward and take her gently by the arm.

"This is not it. This can't be my trailer." Her mouth dropped open as her eyes took in the sparkling blue and white exterior and the darling little outdoor setting they had chosen for her. She shot a glance at them, and for a moment, a hint of moisture showed in her eyes. "Oh no. No. *What* have you all been up to?"

"Molly, go inside!" Tammy said in a fever of impatience. "We've been busting for you to get here, to show you what we've done." She tugged her towards the entrance. "Come on!"

Molly scrambled nimbly into the trailer, speedily demonstrating that her brand-new knees were indeed working perfectly, closely followed by Tammy, Layla, and Georgie. They were not going to miss one second of her reaction.

Molly clasped her hands in front of her while an expression of pure rapture crossed her face. "You…you *tricksters*! I just can't believe it." They watched her, following her gaze, drinking in her reaction as she patted the small, bright red round table, set with polka dot plates in red and white and aqua-colored cups that picked up the hues of the cushions in the seats. "Oh, my stars, what have you done here? You've got the bed made up and still left plenty of room to sit! So clever!" Her eyes rose to a small set of blue corner shelves tucked underneath a broader shelf in white, with a collection of goodies designed to delight her: a pink alarm clock, a miniature hurricane lamp, a tiny bud vase. "I'm never going to leave!" She leaned over the bright quilt, created with patches of red and pink and blue: some sprigged with blossoms and some checked, to stroke the flowered curtains with their cheerful red-checked frill. "My favorite colors. My favorite things." Her head on one side, she stared at the quilt. "Tammy Dyson, you made this, didn't you? I recognize that fabric." She pointed to a square made from joined pieces made in shades of pink and blue. "We spent months making a quilt out of fabric just like this. Where did you *find* this print?"

Tammy grinned, her eyes lighting with pleasure. "I had to put something here that represented the two of us. I knew you'd recognize it. I couldn't believe it when I found fabric that was such a close match."

Molly bit her lip. "I'm not going to cry. I'm not."

"No, don't," Tammy said, her voice catching on

the words. "If you do, I'll start." She hefted the suitcase onto the bed. "Want some help unpacking?"

Georgie caught Layla's eye and inclined her head a fraction. It would be nice to let Tammy and Miss Molly enjoy this moment by themselves. They had quite a bit of history.

"Tams, Layla, and I need to go and help Rosa settle in," she said. "You and Molly come and find us when you're done, OK?"

"That will be in about ten minutes," Molly assured her. "I'm ready to party!"

With a parting glance over her shoulder, smiling at the sight of Miss Molly opening cupboard doors and exclaiming in delight, Georgie followed Layla outside.

"Well," she said, bumping hips with Layla. "I guess you could say that was a success!"

"Worth every second we spent on it," agreed Layla. "It's almost like meeting Tammy's Mom."

"She kind of was a surrogate mom." Tammy had gone to live with an aunt after her mother died, Georgie knew, but it was her aunt's neighbor Miss Molly who had filled the aching void left by the loss of Tammy's mother. "Tams hasn't said a lot about her life, but she has often spoken of Molly."

"When she talks about anyone, it's Molly," Layla agreed. "But getting Tams to talk about her childhood is like trying to open a clam." She nodded to one side. "Rosa is heading this way. Do you want me to help her settle in, or was that just to give Tammy and Molly some time together?"

"No, I can do it. I'll catch up with you soon." With a smile and a nod to people who greeted her, Georgie went to meet her great-grandmother.

One look at her face was enough to tell her something was up. Her brows were lowered over those sharp dark eyes, and her mouth was set in a firm line.

Georgie reached her and touched her arm, staring at her with a slight frown. "Rosa? Is something wrong?"

"Not with me," she said. "But I think Molly is in trouble. We need to talk."

Find it at your preferred bookstore or online:
https://books2read.com/u/3kwRN3

www.ingramcontent.com/pod-product-compliance
Lightning Source LLC
Chambersburg PA
CBHW031418200726
48285CB00017BA/2432